CW01551656

ACKNOWLEDGMENTS

Thank you as always to my rock, Jean, I'd be lost without you in my life.

Special thanks as always go to @studioenp for their superb cover design expertise.

My heartfelt thanks go to my wonderful editor Emmy Ellis, my proofreaders Joseph, Barbara and Jacqueline for spotting all the lingering nits.

Thank you also to my amazing ARC group who help to keep me sane during this process.

To Mary, gone, but never forgotten. I hope you found the peace you were searching for my dear friend.

ALSO BY M A COMLEY

Blind Justice (Novella)

Cruel Justice (Book #1)

Mortal Justice (Novella)

Impeding Justice (Book #2)

Final Justice (Book #3)

Foul Justice (Book #4)

Guaranteed Justice (Book #5)

Ultimate Justice (Book #6)

Virtual Justice (Book #7)

Hostile Justice (Book #8)

Tortured Justice (Book #9)

Rough Justice (Book #10)

Dubious Justice (Book #11)

Calculated Justice (Book #12)

Twisted Justice (Book #13)

Justice at Christmas (Short Story)

Justice at Christmas 2 (novella)

Prime Justice (Book #14)

Heroic Justice (Book #15)

Shameful Justice (Book #16)

Immoral Justice (Book #17)

Toxic Justice (Book #18)

Overdue Justice (Book #19)

Unfair Justice (a 10,000 word short story)

Irrational Justice (a 10,000 word short story)

Seeking Justice (a 15,000 word novella)

Caring For Justice (a 24,000 word novella)

Savage Justice (a 17,000 word novella Featuring THE UNICORN)

Gone In Seconds (Justice Again series #1)

Ultimate Dilemma (Justice Again series #2)

Clever Deception (co-written by Linda S Prather)

Tragic Deception (co-written by Linda S Prather)

Sinful Deception (co-written by Linda S Prather)

Forever Watching You (DI Miranda Carr thriller)

Wrong Place (DI Sally Parker thriller #1)

No Hiding Place (DI Sally Parker thriller #2)

Cold Case (DI Sally Parker thriller#3)

Deadly Encounter (DI Sally Parker thriller #4)

Lost Innocence (DI Sally Parker thriller #5)

Goodbye, My Precious Child (DI Sally Parker #6)

Web of Deceit (DI Sally Parker Novella with Tara Lyons)

The Missing Children (DI Kayli Bright #1)

Killer On The Run (DI Kayli Bright #2)

Hidden Agenda (DI Kayli Bright #3)

Murderous Betrayal (Kayli Bright #4)

Dying Breath (Kayli Bright #5)

Taken (Kayli Bright #6 coming March 2020)

The Hostage Takers (DI Kayli Bright Novella)

No Right to Kill (DI Sara Ramsey #1)

Killer Blow (DI Sara Ramsey #2)

The Dead Can't Speak (DI Sara Ramsey #3)

Deluded (DI Sara Ramsey #4)

The Murder Pact (DI Sara Ramsey #5)

Twisted Revenge (DI Sara Ramsey #6)

The Lies She Told (DI Sara Ramsey #7)

For The Love Of… (DI Sara Ramsey #8)

Run For Your Life (DI Sara Ramsey #9)

Cold Mercy (DI Sara Ramsey #10) Coming Dec 2020

I Know The Truth (A psychological thriller)

The Caller (co-written with Tara Lyons)

Evil In Disguise – a novel based on True events

Deadly Act (Hero series novella)

Torn Apart (Hero series #1)

End Result (Hero series #2)

In Plain Sight (Hero Series #3)

Double Jeopardy (Hero Series #4)

Criminal Actions (Hero Series #5)

Regrets Mean Nothing (Hero #6)

Sole Intention (Intention series #1)

Grave Intention (Intention series #2)

Devious Intention (Intention #3)

Merry Widow (A Lorne Simpkins short story)

It's A Dog's Life (A Lorne Simpkins short story)

A Time To Heal (A Sweet Romance)

A Time For Change (A Sweet Romance)

High Spirits

The Temptation series (Romantic Suspense/New Adult Novellas)

Past Temptation

Lost Temptation

Cozy Mystery Series

Murder at the Wedding

Murder at the Hotel

Murder by the Sea

Tempting Christa (A billionaire romantic suspense co-authored by Tracie Delaney #1)

Avenging Christa (A billionaire romantic suspense co-authored by Tracie Delaney #2)

PROLOGUE

*B*one tired, Nadia removed her uniform and slipped on her jeans and T-shirt. The door opened, and in walked two of her colleagues. "Hi, Jane and Dawn, are you off home now as well?"

"I am," Jane replied.

"No, I have to call in and see how Mum's getting on. She had her hip operation last week and is suffering, so I said I'd go around there and have a look, make sure she's healing properly," Dawn said.

"That's the trouble, we're never really off duty, are we?"

"You can say that again, Nadia. Have you got any plans for the evening?" Jane asked.

She shook her head and smiled. "No, except to settle down with a nice glass of wine and an omelette. Then go to bed and get ready to start all over again tomorrow."

"Go on, you might complain to us about the job but you love it really. What else would we do?"

Nadia contemplated the question for a few seconds before she responded, "Pass. I'm not one of those girls who could throw themselves at the mercy of a rich man. It would do my head in, sitting around preening myself all day, waiting for him to come home and take advantage of me."

"You are funny. I bet there'd be certain fringe benefits to living a life like that," Jane said, a twinkle in her eye. She'd recently broken up with her fella after living with him for over ten years.

"I suppose it depends what you want out of life," Nadia said thoughtfully.

Both women nodded.

"We're going to have to go out on the town together soon, ladies, we obviously need to put the world to rights over a drink or two." Dawn gave them both a cheeky wink.

"We'll sort something out in the next few days. I think I'm working a few extra shifts this week, so it would have to be either next week or the week after."

"We'll get something organised. Enjoy your relaxing evening, Nadia."

"Thanks, you, too. See you in the morning."

She waved goodbye and left the locker room to begin the long walk through the hospital corridors down to the car park. There were fewer people around at this time of night. Visiting hours had finished long ago, and they were starting the graveyard shift as most of the staff called it. Anything after ten was deemed that, and it was already ten past by the time she stepped through the main entrance. Fortunately, she made it to the car without being side-tracked by any other members of staff.

Nadia crossed the road to the designated staff car park and pressed the key fob to open her Mini. It was a rust bucket but went well and had never let her down. She'd had her eye on a new car but there was no way she'd be able to afford the extortionate payments on a loan, not on her meagre wage, and there was no way she would ask her father to chip in. He'd made it perfectly clear years ago, that once she started earning money for a living she was on her own. That suited her. If she couldn't afford something, she never bought it. She had no debts, and her bank balance had a couple of hundred sitting in it at the end of the month. Talking to her friends, not many of them could say that.

Most of her friends were sinking in a whirlpool of debt just so they had bragging rights to owning the latest cars and, in some cases, designer outfits. Not her. She was plain old Nadia, risk averse and happy to plod along in life.

The right man had failed to come her way. At twenty-eight, most women would be panicking about not having a band of gold on their finger, but not her. All right, she couldn't say she enjoyed her life as it was, but she was better off than most women she knew. She had a roof over her head and a career she loved.

She drove towards home and turned up the radio when one of her favourite songs came on. She loved Michael Bolton, had even splashed out on a ticket to see him up in Birmingham a few years back on his sell-out tour of the UK.

The day's anxieties drifted away during the drive. She was looking forward to opening the bottle of wine she'd spoken about with Dawn and Jane. Her father would be watching some action movie or other on Netflix in the lounge. That didn't bother her. She'd rustle up her omelette and take it upstairs, eat it in her bedroom while catching up on the soaps she'd recorded that had aired earlier on in the evening.

The light was on in the lounge, and there was a gap in the curtain, one of her pet hates, and her blood boiled. Her father usually did that just to annoy her. She exited the car and made her way towards the house. She slotted her key in the lock. The TV was blaring as usual. She called out, but her father either ignored her intentionally or hadn't heard above the din. After slipping off her shoes, she pushed open the lounge door. "Dad, do you have to... Dad, no, are you all right?"

Her father was lying on the floor, blood soaking into the cream carpet all around him. It was up the walls and all over the matching cream leather sofa. Tears stung her eyes, and her throat clogged up. *Calm, keep calm. Do what you need to do to make sure he survives.* She gently shook his shoulder and then tore off her jacket and pressed down on the gaping wound to his throat.

"Dad, please, stay with me." She reached for her handbag and fished out her mobile to ring nine-nine-nine. "Yes, I need an ambulance at seven Rotherhide Close. It's my father, he's been attacked in our house... I'm a nurse, I've just finished my shift and found him like this. Get an ambulance, please hurry."

"Don't worry, one is on its way. You know what to do or do you need me to see you through the procedure?" the woman at the control centre asked.

"No. I know. Please hurry, he's lost so much blood. Shit, he's not going to make it."

"Hang in there. The ambulance is a few minutes away."

"Dad, they're on their way. Don't you dare fall asleep, you hear me?"

A few minutes later sirens wailed in the distance. She shifted her father's head off her lap, opened the front door and urged the paramedics to hurry. She led the two men into the living room. They took over, assessed his vital signs and injected him with morphine.

"What's your name, love?"

"It's Nadia. I'm a nurse. I did what I could to stop the bleeding. Please, you have to save him."

"He's more comfortable now. We'll take him to the hospital, they'll be able to tend to his wounds better there. Do you want to come with us or stay here and talk to the police?"

"The police? No, I need to stay with Dad, he needs me, the police can wait."

The paramedic with the brown hair nodded and asked his colleague to fetch the stretcher. The other man shot out of the room.

While he was gone, the paramedic with the brown hair asked, "What happened?"

"I don't know. I've been on shift all day. He was like this when I got home. Will he make it? Look at all the blood he's lost." She pointed at the huge amount covering the sofa.

"We'll have to wait and see. Stay positive, these things have a habit of working out for the best."

"I wish I had your faith."

"Has he spoken to you?"

"No."

"Don't worry. Let's get him to the hospital and go from there. Do you need to call a member of your family?"

"I don't want to worry my sister, not until I know the outcome. Oh

God. Dad, please be all right." She touched his cheek with a feather-light caress.

The paramedics lifted his unresponsive body onto the stretcher. Nadia hurriedly checked around the house, collected her bag, made sure her phone was inside and followed the men out to the ambulance.

"Do you want to hop in the back or bring your own car?"

"I'll come with you, if that's okay?"

"Of course. Jump in." Her hand shook as she reached out for her father's gnarled fingers. Arthritis had set in a few years ago. He was only fifty-five but had worked with his hands all his life. He was a carpenter for a local sawmill.

"Dad, Dad, can you hear me? Squeeze my hand if you can hear me."

He groaned, but his eyes remained closed, a pained expression twisting his features. Her heart felt heavy. She wished she could rid him of the pain.

The ambulance got under way and started up its siren once more. The noise blocked out any further attempt of Nadia speaking to her father.

Her sister's face drifted into her mind. She'd be distraught by the news if he didn't pull through. *Stop thinking that way, of course he's going to make it. But all that blood...can he really survive losing that amount?*

The voices in her head went back and forth until the ambulance drew to a halt outside Accident and Emergency. Her father was whisked through the corridors, the paramedic giving the awaiting doctor and nurses the facts about his vital signs.

"Nadia, what are you doing here?" Maureen, the nurse, asked.

"He's my dad, please, do your best for him."

"Oh my...of course we will. You'd better wait in the family room. Let the doctor give him the once-over, he'll come and see you soon."

Nadia stopped dead. "Can't I go with him?" She reached out a shaking hand.

"No, you know you can't. The doctor will drop by and see you soon," Maureen insisted.

Nadia stood and watched her colleagues push her father up the corridor. Hopelessness descended and cast a cloud over her. Her shoulders slouched, and she made her way to the family room at the end of the hallway. It had recently been brightly painted to help ease the waiting families' doom and gloom.

She picked up a magazine to distract herself, flipping through the pages. None of it registered. Her mind lay elsewhere, with her father. *What will I do if he dies?* She mentally kicked herself for asking the question.

She glanced at her watch numerous times over the next thirty minutes or so, until the doctor finally came to give her the news she'd been waiting for.

"Nadia, you don't know me, I'm Doctor Morgan. I'm going to give it to you straight. Your father is a very ill man. To be honest, we're unsure whether he'll make it or not. We're in the process of giving him a blood transfusion. Does he have any illnesses we should know about that could possibly hamper his recovery?"

"No, nothing, he's always been fairly fit."

"I see. Well, that should make his recovery straightforward then. He'll be going down to surgery to repair the damage to his neck soon."

"Thank you, Doctor. What you're really saying is not to count my chickens just yet, right?"

"Correct. I always err on the side of caution. You'd do well to do the same, for now. You don't need me to tell you he's in safe hands. Try and get some rest. Would you rather go home and we'll call you with an update?"

"No, I'm going nowhere, not until I know he's going to be all right."

The doctor left the room. She collapsed into the chair and covered her face with her hands, unable to hold back the river of tears that flowed for the next ten minutes. Her fighting spirit deserted her for the time being. Once her tears had dried up, she thrust back her shoulders and turned her gloomy thoughts to more positive ones, promising only to look on the brighter side of the predicament she and her father found themselves in.

But one question remained prominent in her mind…who did this? Two actually: who and why? Why would anyone attempt to take her father's life in such a callous way? Was it an intruder? How did they get in?

The doctor came to get her an hour later. By that time, her mind was as tired as her body had been when she'd left work almost two hours before. He escorted her to the recovery room where she held her father's hand until she drifted off to sleep.

She was awoken by the sound of the ventilator alarm going off. She shot out of the chair and hovered over him. "Dad, Dad, stay with us."

His eyes flickered open. She squeezed his hand and bent her head to listen to what he was attempting to say.

"I didn't mean to do it…"

"Dad, do what?"

The machine flatlined.

He'd gone.

1

———————

*K*aty and Charlie said farewell and left the station. They hadn't even reached their cars before the night desk sergeant bellowed for them to return. Katy made a point of looking at her watch. It was gone midnight—she and her partner had already put in a fifteen-hour shift and were both exhausted.

The sergeant shrugged. "Sorry, ma'am, thought you'd want to hear about this one."

"Go on, I'm waiting with bated breath."

Charlie sniggered. "I'm fine, don't worry about me."

Katy turned to look at her. "For the record, I wasn't. I was more concerned about getting home to my saint of a husband."

"Oh right, yes, of course," Charlie mumbled.

Katy thumped her arm. "Stop feeling sorry for yourself. I can handle it if you want to go home."

"No way. It would be playing on my mind anyway, so I might as well stick around."

"Now that's settled…" Ray said. "We received a call a few hours ago about a man having his throat cut. I didn't bother you about it back then in case it didn't come to anything, but now…"

"Don't tell me, the guy has since died, hence you getting the Murder Squad involved."

"Exactly. The hospital called it in. The daughter is still over there with him."

"Still? Was she there when the attack took place?" Katy queried.

"Apparently she rang for an ambulance after coming home from work and finding her father in that state."

"Interesting. We'll drop by and see her. Do we know what ward?"

"Her father had just had an operation and was in the recovery room, I believe."

"We'll find them. Thanks, Ray. What's the name?"

"The victim is Bruce Crawford, his daughter is Nadia."

"Thanks again. We'll take my car, Charlie."

They arrived at the hospital around ten minutes later and parked in one of the numerous available spaces.

"Makes a change not to be hunting for a space around here, I'll see that as a good omen." Katy got out of the car and jabbed the fob to lock it once Charlie had joined her.

"If you say so. Nothing about this seems 'good' to me," Charlie muttered.

"I hear you. Let's see if the daughter is up to speaking to us. I doubt it. If she's not, we can arrange to call round to see her in the morning and trundle off home to bed."

"Wishful thinking on your part, I fear," Charlie said with a grin.

"We'll see. I'll ask at reception where we're likely to find her."

The receptionist furnished them with lengthy directions which Katy lost halfway through. She smiled and thanked the woman, and they set off. "I hope you remembered the latter part of those instructions because she lost me after the seventh right turn."

Charlie grinned. "Yep, don't worry."

There was a nurse exiting the room when they eventually found it.

Katy flashed her ID. "Hi, we're looking for a Miss Crawford. Is she in there?"

"She is. I'm not sure she's in any fit state to talk to the police, though."

"We'll be gentle with her, I promise. Is it all right if we go in?"

"I suppose so." The woman spun on her heel and dashed up the corridor.

Katy inhaled a few deep breaths and entered the room. There was a young woman sitting beside a man who was obviously no longer alive.

Katy was shocked to see him lying there uncovered. "Hello, Miss Crawford, is it? Sorry for the intrusion."

The woman slowly turned to look at them. "Yes. Who are you? No, please, don't take him away from me, not yet. I haven't had the chance to say goodbye to him properly. I've just been sitting here numb…"

"I can understand that. No, we haven't come to take him away. I'm DI Katy Foster, and this is my partner, DC Charlie Simpkins from the Met Police. Would it be possible to have a word with you?"

"Now? Right *now*, you expect me to answer your questions?"

"Just a few, if you don't mind." Katy studied the woman. Her clothes were covered in blood, which could only mean one thing: she'd probably contaminated the scene back at the house. Or there could be another scenario for her to consider, that the woman was the perpetrator. She'd come across cases like that in the past. It wasn't beyond the realms of possibility, nothing was in this day and age. Not when the perps seemed to be getting cannier by the day.

Nadia let out a shuddering breath. "If you must. I'm not leaving this room, you can say what you have to say right here."

"That's all right. Can you tell us what happened?"

The sergeant had given them a brief rundown of events, but Katy wanted to see if the woman came up with the same account of what had gone on.

"I came home from work just after ten-twenty and found him lying on the living room floor. I tried my hardest to help him."

"You touched him?"

The woman glanced up, seemingly appalled by the question. "Of course, what would you have done in the same situation?"

Katy acknowledged Nadia's rebuttal was probably a valid one. "You're right. Go on."

"I'm a nurse, if that helps you to assess things more accurately. I took an oath to help those in distress or injured."

"Ah, well, that definitely sheds a different light on things. Thanks. Was there anyone else in the house when you got home?"

"No. I only managed to search the house briefly while the paramedics worked on him and couldn't find anything wrong. The back door was shut. I think the front door was closed when I got there, I would have remembered if it hadn't been."

"Was your father due to see anyone this evening?"

"No, he rarely goes out or accepts visitors, not nowadays. He goes to work and that's it. He had heart problems and was awaiting a bypass." She stared at her father's snow-white face and ran her hand down his cheek. "Maybe he didn't have the strength to fight back. Had he been twenty years younger he would've throttled the person before they had a chance to lay a finger on him."

"Did you live with your father?" Katy needed to ask the question. She reckoned Nadia was in her late twenties to early thirties, which seemed old for a young woman to be at home still.

"Is there a law against that?" Nadia bit back defensively.

"No, it wasn't a judgement, just an enquiry into why you were at the house, really."

Nadia's gaze fell on her father once more. "I see. Yes, I've always lived with my father. Have you seen the price of property in the area? Out of my reach on my paltry nurse's salary."

"Yes, I get that. What about your mother, is she still with you?"

Her gaze lowered to her hands. "No. My mother died when I was four and my sister was three."

"Sister? Does she live with you as well?"

"No, Penny has her own life up in Scotland. She's married to Adam; he works on the oil rigs up there."

"Do you see her much?"

"Not as often as I'd like. I've rung her, she's on her way to be with me. She's promised to help me with the funeral arrangements. I've never had to deal with any of this crap before and I wouldn't know where to start." Tears dripped onto her flushed cheeks.

"It's difficult losing a loved one, grieving and doing all that's necessary for their funeral. Don't you have anyone local who can help you? Relatives or close friends?"

"No, Penny will be here tomorrow. We'll bounce some ideas around between us, she's far more organised than me. I'm sure she'll have it all figured out within a few hours."

"That'll help take the pressure off your shoulders."

"That's what I thought. I miss her, it'll be nice seeing her again, even if it is in these dreadful circumstances. I can't believe he's gone. I thought they might be able to save him. The surgeon told me the wound was very deep and had severed his voice box and even nicked his cervical spinal cord, so I doubt he would've been able to walk again even if he had survived the attack."

"Sorry to hear that." Katy was tempted to add that maybe it was a good job he hadn't survived with such debilitating injuries, but kept her mouth shut instead, unsure how callous that might have sounded, coming from a complete stranger.

"The whole thing is a mess. Why kill him? He's never done anyone any harm, not from what I can remember." Nadia's shoulders shook as her grief overwhelmed her again.

Katy took a step closer to the bed to try to comfort Nadia, but she pulled away. "Would you rather we leave this until the morning?"

"No. I'm on duty at nine, doing a twelve-hour shift. We're short-staffed, I refuse to let my colleagues down."

"You can't work, it's too soon. You need time to come to terms with your loss first. I'm sure your bosses will understand, in the circumstances."

"You don't understand, I want to work. What else would I do? Sit and stare at the four walls of our lounge? That reminds me…" She stood and placed her chair against the wall behind her. "I need to go home, to clean up, ready for when Penny arrives."

Katy raised a hand. "Hold on a second, I'm afraid you won't be able to do that. Your house is a crime scene. SOCO will need to examine it thoroughly, searching for clues to tell us who did this to your father. You'll be allowed to gather some personal belongings to see you through the next few days. If you don't have any relatives or friends you can stay with then my suggestion would be for you to get a hotel room for at least two days."

"Great, as if I have funds for that. Maybe I'll do my long shifts here and then crash in my car. That's all I'm likely to be able to afford. Can't you section the house off? I promise not to go in the living room, if that's what you want."

"It's not as simple as that. I'm sorry for any inconvenience caused, needs must, I'm afraid. Every surface will have to be examined and analysed if we're to secure a conviction against the person responsible. I know that's an inconvenience to you."

"It is what it is. I don't want to cause any trouble. I'm sorry if it came across that way."

"It didn't. Why don't we take you home now, so you can pick up some of your belongings, and then we can drop you off at a hotel?"

She shook her head. "No, I don't want that. Yes, I'll go back to the house to gather some clothes and essentials I need but I refuse to waste money on a hotel room."

"I hate to say this, but what about your sister? You can't expect her to sleep in your car, can you?"

"She can sort herself out when she gets here. I shouldn't have to make her arrangements for her. Bloody hell, I've just lost my father, don't do this to me. All I want to do is sit here with him, and you're causing all this anxiety. I. Don't. Want. It."

"Okay, would you rather we leave you alone? It's late, we can complete the questioning tomorrow, if you'd rather."

"Say what you need to say and leave me alone. Isn't your job to be out there looking for the vile person who did this to him?"

"Of course it is, and we'll get around to doing that once we have a clearer indication of what we're searching for. At the moment, we have nothing."

Nadia grunted and held her arms out to the sides. "Are you blaming me for that?"

"No, I really wasn't. Nadia, we're on your side here. I'm sorry if you've misunderstood what I've said. My intention was to try and ease your burden."

"No, it should be *me* who is apologising. It's the grief talking. I'm not usually snappy, my colleagues will tell you that. All this is too much. To find my father in that state, to sit around here for a few hours, waiting to hear news, and for him to come out of surgery only to go and die on me. I guess the stress has just got the better of me."

"It's fine. It's also extremely late. I can pay for a hotel room for the night, if that will help you out?"

Nadia gasped and swept her hand, still spattered in dry blood, through her long auburn hair. "I'm not a charity case. I can rob Peter to pay Paul if necessary. The thing is, I shouldn't need to. Not when I have a perfectly good house waiting for me."

"In our defence, a house which is running alive with forensic technicians in an attempt to find your father's killer swiftly."

"There's no easy solution. I'll be fine. I can see if there's a room available in the nurses' quarters attached to the hospital."

"If you're sure."

"I am. I'm tired now, can we put an end to all this?"

"Sure. I'll leave you my card, in the hope you get in touch with me if you can remember anything else about what happened during the incident that you believe we should be interested in."

Nadia took the card and tucked it in her small handbag nestled on the floor beside her. "Thank you. Again, I apologise if I've come across obstructive and unhelpful. I have truly told you everything I know about what happened tonight."

"We'll leave you to it and be in touch soon. Sorry, would it be okay if we get a contact number for you?"

Nadia reeled off her mobile number, and Charlie jotted it down in her notebook. "It's mostly turned off because of the length of time I'm at work, so please be patient if you try to contact me and there's a delay in me getting back to you. It won't be intentional, I swear."

"I have no reason to doubt you. We're sorry for your loss, you have our sincere condolences. Take care of yourself. We'll be in touch soon."

"Thank you for being so understanding, both of you."

Katy and Charlie left the room.

Outside, Katy exhaled a large breath. "Shit! I hate dealing with grieving relatives." She raised a hand to prevent Charlie from answering. "I know what you're about to say, most of our job entails just that…well, I'm stating, here and now, that I categorically abhor that side of our job."

"It's not easy, I grant you. But you handled yourself well in there, just saying."

"Charlie Simpkins, are you sucking up to me?"

Charlie placed a hand over her chest. "Would I? By the way, I thought it was very magnanimous of you to offer to pay for a hotel room."

"Ooo, such a big word for this early in the morning." She glanced at her watch to check the time and nodded. "Jesus, it's almost two, hardly worth going home, is it? Oh, and for your information, I wouldn't have footed the bill personally, I would have taken it out of the petty cash tin."

"Ah, thought it sounded too good to be true."

Katy swiped at Charlie's arm. "Sodding cheek. Okay, let's call it a day and get home. I'll drop you back at the station first."

"We should have thought about that and brought both cars. You're not going out of your way, are you? If you are, I can grab a taxi from the rank, there's sure to be a few outside."

"Now you're being downright silly. Come on."

They set off back to the car, neither of them choosing to speak about the case on the way.

Once they were in the car Katy asked, "What did you make of her?"

"Nadia? Why, don't tell me you have suspicions about her?"

Katy waggled her hand in front of her and then slipped the key into the ignition. "I'm not sure about her. Yes, I felt sorry for her for losing her father, but did you see the state of her clothes?"

"About that...shouldn't we have taken them for analysis?"

"You're right, I didn't have the heart to ask her to strip off while we were there. My mistake. I'll take the rap for that with Patti in the morning. I'll get SOCO to contact her and ask for her clothes. Come on, what's your gut telling you?"

Charlie puffed out her cheeks then chewed on her lip for a few moments. "I don't know, it's hard to say. She's a nurse, so her story about trying to save him is plausible, I suppose."

"If you found a member of your family bleeding out like that, I'm guessing you'd react in the same way, right?"

"Without a doubt. Not everyone has the time to stop and think about their dubious actions, do they?"

"True enough. It's going to add to SOCO's burden, there's no doubt about that."

"Yeah, I think you're right. However, the fact she still lives with her father struck me as strange. What about you?"

"Yes and no. She has a point, property prices are the pits in the London area. It's the same for everyone, young and old."

"We'll discuss it more in the morning. I'm shagged and need some kip."

Ten minutes later, after dropping Charlie off, Katy was heading in the opposite direction towards home. She parked the car and snuck into the house. A light was on, seeping under the lounge door, and she eased it open to find AJ fast asleep on the couch. She ran a hand down his cheek. His eyelids flickered.

"Hello, you. What are you doing up?"

"Silly question. What time is it?"

"I stopped looking at the clock around two, it was depressing me. Come on, let's go to bed. I need a cuddle."

He gathered the quilt and pillow and followed her upstairs. When she came out of the en suite, he was fast asleep again. She refused to wake him a second time so crept in beside him and drifted off to sleep as soon as she was warm and cosy.

2

_____

As soon as Katy arrived at the station, she arranged for SOCO to contact Nadia about her clothes. She gave James the young woman's number and warned him to be gentle with her.

"What do you take me for? Of course I'll be gentle. Is she a suspect?"

"Good, and no, not at this point. I'm inclined to think she was acting on second nature, what with her being a full-time nurse."

"Ah, I'm with you. Okay, leave it with me."

"Thanks."

She ended the call, and before she got stuck into tackling the daily grind of sorting through the morning post, she called a meeting with the team. "Right, guys, this is what we have so far. According to the victim's daughter, Nadia Crawford, she came home from work to find her father lying in a pool of blood on the living room floor. His throat had been cut. She's a nurse, so her first instinct was to try and save him. Her second was to call for an ambulance. Charlie and I were with her until gone two this morning. She was traumatised by the events, which is totally understandable. However, me being cautious to cover every angle, I think we should begin background checks on the father and the daughter."

Katy wrote both names on the whiteboard. "I want a couple of you to go out there and conduct house-to-house enquiries—all we can hope is that a neighbour saw something. Nadia came home around ten-twenty, I believe, so any time before that. Thinking about it, with his injuries, he wouldn't have lasted too long. So let's narrow it down to between nine and ten, although I'm thinking more along the lines of nine-thirty. I know, I'm waffling as I'm thinking out loud. Who's up for the task?"

Patrick and Stephen raised their hands.

"Thanks, guys. That's all I've got to tell you at present. Wait, I'll contact Nadia. She wanted to get some personal belongings from the house. While you're there, have a word with SOCO and oversee accompanying her inside to pick up her stuff for me, would you?"

"Sure. Where's she going to stay? Does she have relatives in the area?" Patrick asked.

"No. I think I've persuaded her to stay in a hotel. Her sister is travelling down from Scotland, haven't got a clue when she's likely to show up. I'll ring Nadia and get back to you."

Katy entered her office to make the call. She stood by the window overlooking the car park at the front of the station. "Hi, Nadia, it's DI Katy Foster. How are you feeling today?"

The woman sighed and yawned. "Sorry about that. I'm okay. I've just got up, I'm getting ready to go into work."

"What? Well, I would advise against you doing that. You must still be in shock, that's going to affect the way you carry out your job."

"I need to be around people. I need the interaction. If I sit in a hotel room I'm going to go out of my mind."

"What about your sister? Isn't she due to join you today?"

"She's due this afternoon, getting in around three. I'll take time off to get her settled at the hotel and return to work. Please, don't question my actions. I need to be busy, to be distracted. I've barely slept all night. Every time I closed my eyes...I saw my father's throat cut open..."

"I'm sorry about that, Nadia. I can't profess to know what being confronted with such a horrendous ordeal can do to a person. I can arrange for you to see a counsellor, if that's what you want or need to get through this."

"I don't know what I want. What I need is my father back, but the likelihood of that happening is non-existent."

"It is. I still don't think you're doing the right thing by going into work. Is your immediate supervisor aware of the situation?"

"Yes, the ward sister understands my reasons for going in and has given me the all clear, under the proviso that if things turn out to be too tough to deal with, I leave and go back to the hotel."

Katy found that piece of news incredulous, especially as Nadia would be dealing with patients on the ward, effectively putting their lives at risk if her thoughts lay elsewhere. "Oh, I see. A couple of my officers will be out at the house today, conducting house-to-house enquiries with the neighbouring property owners. I know you said you wanted to grab some personal effects from your home; they can oversee that if you want, today."

"Oh, yes. That'd be good. What time will they be there?"

"They'll be leaving soon. Should be there in about twenty minutes, does that suit you?"

"Yes, I don't have to be at work until ten, so that's perfect. I can snatch a change of clothes and pack a bag of essentials, and then go straight to work. Thank you."

"You're welcome. I'll let my boys know to expect you. I'll be in touch soon. Don't forget to call if you need to speak to me."

"I won't. Will you do the same if you find out who…killed my father?"

"Without hesitation. Speak soon." Katy ended the call and returned to the incident room. "Guys, I'd leave now. I've told Nadia you'll be there in twenty minutes. You know what to do when you enter the house. Suit up, including her, and escort her to her room. Don't allow her to roam around the house unattended."

"Yes, boss," Patrick replied. He got to his feet and left the room with Stephen.

"Okay, that's them sorted. What's left for you guys to do? It's a residential area, so no chance of obtaining any CCTV footage for the road in which they live. Our only hope is that one of the neighbours comes up trumps. Karen, if you can begin the background checks for me."

"Already started on them, boss. Do you want their bank accounts checked as well?"

"If you would. Charlie, can you see what the system throws up for any crimes of this nature taking place, or armed robberies—we can't discount that theory either—within a twenty-mile radius in the past two months? I'm guessing there won't be; however, at this stage of the investigation, there's really nothing else for us to tackle."

"What about calling a press conference?" Charlie suggested.

"The thought crossed my mind. I think it's a bit early to consider holding one just yet. Let's see what the boys come up with. Karen, will you add the sister to your list? Although, I don't know her married name. Her Christian name is Penny."

"Leave it with me."

"I'll be in my office." She stopped off at the vending machine and took a cup of coffee with her. Her mind was numb, and she found herself staring at the unopened letters piled on her desk, not having the heart to open them. Instead, she decided to ring Patti. "Hi, sorry to disturb you. I don't suppose you've had a chance to perform the PM yet?"

"Good morning to you, too, Katy. You'd be right in your thinking. I've only been at work for an hour, give me a break."

"Sorry, eager to know what your take on the vic is."

"Why? You're not usually one for chasing things up so early. Is there something you need to get off your chest?"

"To be honest, I can't explain it. I know Lorne used to go on about working on her gut instinct and I always pooh-poohed it, maybe that's what I'm dealing with now. Something just isn't sitting comfortably with me, and I can't seem to put my finger on what it is. Am I making any bloody sense at all?"

"Yes and no. What are your reservations?"

"The daughter. You're aware she called it in, aren't you?"

"I am. Hmm…it's too early for me to make a judgement call just yet. Wasn't she with him at the hospital?"

"Yes. See, that's where I begin to doubt myself. She's a bloody nurse, her instinct would be to try and help her father, right?"

"You'd think so. Are you telling me she didn't do that? Only, that's different to what I heard."

"No, she did. But surely, wouldn't she know better than to get stuck in?"

"My honest opinion is that I think you're probably reading too much into it. If she's a nurse then it would be in her nature to try and help him all she could, wouldn't it?"

"I suppose so. Maybe I'm guilty of overthinking the situation."

"Probably. Want to join me for the PM?"

"I do and I don't. Go on then. What time are you going to start?"

"Within ten minutes. I can delay it a few minutes, give you time to get here, if that's what you want?"

"I'll leave now. Thanks, for listening and not thinking I'm a nutter."

"Nonsense. We all get cases that challenge us now and again. Mark this one down as your thorn-in-the-side case."

"See you soon." She rushed out of the office and stopped at Charlie's desk. "I'm going to attend the PM. Do you want to leave what you're doing and come with me, or would you rather give this one a miss?"

"I'm easy either way. You're the boss, you tell me."

"Leave that and come with me. We'll be back soon, Karen. If you hear anything from the boys, ring me, okay?"

"I will. Erm…have fun." Karen grimaced as the words tumbled out of her mouth.

Katy smiled and shook her head. "I doubt it."

*S*uited in operating greens and half-wellies, Katy and Charlie joined Patti in the examination suite. "Good to see you both again. You're just in time to see the first cut."

Katy cringed. "I was hoping you'd have him opened up by now."

Patti grinned. "Thought I'd delay it until you arrived. Here we go, ladies."

Katy's legs trembled slightly as Patti made the first cut. She faced Charlie who was straining her neck to see what was going on. "You're warped."

Charlie sniggered. "And there was you thinking I wouldn't enjoy this side of things."

Patti glanced up. "Just like your mother. She was always the first to step forward and take note of what I was doing with a scalpel."

"I didn't know that," Charlie replied, her gaze fixed on the blade while it carved out the Y-incision.

"Okay, let's see what we've got here. The cut to the throat was clean, no jagged edges in sight, therefore, the knife used would've had a straight edge. The cut was deep and severed his larynx."

"What does that tell you, if anything?" Katy asked.

"My first inclination would be that the cut was made in anger."

"Interesting."

"What if this was a burglary? The perp would have been livid to find someone in the property, wouldn't they?" Charlie piped up.

Katy nodded and rotated her head to relieve the tension in her neck. "True enough."

"Shall I continue?" Patti asked.

"Please do."

"From what I can tell there are no other wounds to the body. To me, that would suggest the perpetrator only had one intention: to kill the man. Would a burglar set out to do that?"

"Maybe, maybe not," Katy said, her mind whirling. "Maybe he had an enemy, someone his daughter isn't aware of, who wanted shot of him."

"That's for you to find out. Let me continue." Patti carried on with her examination. She assessed the internal organs and gave them a full rundown of what she found. "His liver shows signs of excessive drinking. His lungs aren't faring any better, heavy smoker, I'm guessing. I suspect he had a heart problem judging by the state of his valves."

"Most men are at that age, aren't they? Or is that me being presumptuous?"

"Not *all* men, but a vast majority, I have to agree. There are a few bruises on his lower legs. They're old contusions, at least a week old, so not related to his murder. Ah, what's this...?" Patti leaned in closer to the man's stomach. She glanced up at Katy. "You'll need to check his medical records, but I think you'll find he was dying of stomach cancer."

"Really? I wonder why Nadia didn't mention that," Katy said.

"Who knows? It's a significant mass. He must have been in a lot of pain. Maybe he hid it from her."

"Something I need to check with her all the same. Nadia lived with him. Surely, she would have noticed if he was in pain or not, wouldn't she?"

"Possibly. In her defence, you know what most men are like when they're ill. Again, check with his doctor, see if he was being treated first before your mind wanders into unknown territory."

"I will, don't worry. I wonder if the perp knew he was dying. Ignore me, a rhetorical question. The plot thickens, right? Anything else, Patti?"

"Nope, I think we're about finished here."

"Good. Okay, we'll leave you to complete it in peace."

Patti nodded and got back to work.

Katy and Charlie ditched their greens and wellies and left the hospital. "We need to find out who his doctor was. I don't really want to ring the daughter again."

"Want me to call all the surgeries in the area?"

"If you would."

Charlie got down to the task and immediately hit the jackpot with the third call she made. "The receptionist is patching me through to the doctor now. Do you want to take over?"

"No, you deal with it. Ask him how long he's had the cancer. What treatment he's had for it. Whether he was taking any medication, and then finally, ask him if his daughter, Nadia, was aware of his illness. Put it on speaker so I can hear what he has to say."

"Will do. Ah, yes, Doctor Malik, I wonder if you can help me. We're conducting a murder enquiry and believe the victim to be one of your patients. Bruce Crawford."

"Yes my receptionist told me that's why you're calling. It's very sad to hear he's no longer with us. How can I help?"

"You're aware he had stomach cancer, I take it?"

"Yes. I diagnosed his condition over six months ago. He was a poorly man. Didn't have long to live. No, you don't think he killed himself, do you? No, you said something about a murder enquiry, I forgot that."

"That's right, it's hard to take the news in sometimes. Can I ask what treatment he was undergoing? And were you aware he was still working?"

"He's recently completed a course of chemo—it wasn't successful. I gave him the news that he only had three months at the longest to live when he came to see me last week. He was understandably devastated by the news, as you can imagine and yes, he wanted to keep working, rather than sit at home, waiting for his dying day to arrive."

"Can you tell me if his daughter was aware of his condition?"

"Nadia? No, she wasn't. He refused to let me tell her. I told him I wouldn't go against his wishes but urged him to tell her himself. She's a nurse and would have cared for him, if he'd been willing to confide in her."

"Did he give a reason why he didn't want to inform her?" Charlie asked.

"No. Actually, he said he'd lived his life and didn't want to become a burden to his two daughters. I had to stand by his wishes, my hands were tied."

"I see." Charlie glanced at Katy and whispered, "Anything else?"

Katy shook her head. "No, that's fine."

"Thank you for taking my call, Doctor, and for giving me the information."

"No problem."

Charlie hit the End Call button and placed the phone in her lap.

"Strange he kept his cancer a secret from his kids, especially if

Nadia is a nurse. Katy pulled up at a red light and drummed her fingers on the steering wheel.

"Seems odd, doesn't it? I can't get my head around it. It sounds to me like he just gave up."

"That's my take on it, too. Why? Because he'd lived his life and was fed up with it? Hard to contemplate anyone wanting to give in to the disease like that."

"He'd gone through the chemo. I've heard that can take a dreadful toll on a body." Charlie shuddered.

"Yeah, again, it doesn't add up. Surely Nadia would have known about the chemo."

"Hmm…maybe it was carried out at a different hospital."

The light turned green, and Katy put her foot on the accelerator. "I know it's the wrong time to grill her, but we could do with sitting Nadia down and doing just that."

"We'd be quite within our rights to question her again, wouldn't we? Or am I missing something as a newbie?" Charlie asked, her brow pulling into a deep frown.

"No, you're right. Maybe it's me being a tad cautious. Treating the woman with respect, knowing that she's grieving."

"I understand that, but if you have doubts about her story then maybe you should dive in and get some answers."

"I hear what you're saying. Let's hold back a while, see what the boys come up with first. Actually, I'm going to chase them up, find out if they have any news for us." She indicated and drove into a nearby parking space and made the call.

Patrick answered on the second ring. "Hello, boss, anything up?"

"Not really. How are things progressing there?"

"Slowly. Nadia turned up around thirty minutes ago. I accompanied her into the house, and she left not long after."

"How did she seem to you?"

Patrick groaned. "Dazed and confused. Going through the motions, I suppose."

"I see. I'm going through the mill here. Pondering whether to call her in for questioning or not."

"Any particular reason, boss?"

"In my eyes, there are a lot of things that simply aren't adding up. Did she say anything to you at all?"

"No. She was desperate to step into the lounge for some personal effects. I told her she couldn't. She begged me to go in there to collect a family photo for her. I looked for the particular one she mentioned, but the frame was empty. She broke down and cried when I told her that."

"Wait, back up a minute. There was an empty photo frame and she wasn't aware that it was empty?"

"That's right. I asked her when she noticed the last time the frame was full, and she said yesterday before she went to work."

"Hmm...now that is weird. Why would someone break into the house, remove one of the photos and then kill her father, or do it the other way around? Bloody hell, what are we up against here? During the PM, we discovered that Bruce only had a few weeks or months to live. He had stomach cancer. We chased it up with the doctor, and he told us that neither Nadia nor her sister were aware of his illness."

"Wow, that's strange. If Nadia's a nurse, wouldn't she have recognised the signs if he was terminally ill?"

"My thoughts exactly. The poor man had to go through months of chemo as well."

"Jesus. She had to have known, surely?"

"I'm going to try and have another word with her. I take it she was on her way into work after leaving you guys."

"She was. She packed a holdall and was in and out within ten minutes tops. I asked her if she needed a lift or anything else, and she mumbled that she had it covered and to leave her alone to get on with her life."

"Odd thing to say when someone offers you help. Maybe we'll leave her alone today and chase her up again tomorrow, once the sister has arrived. Hang on, were there any other photos of the family in the lounge?"

"Yes, a few. Why?"

"If you get the chance to either go back inside the house or to speak to a SOCO, ask them to take a shot of the photos, just so I know what we're dealing with."

"Okay. Is there anything else you need?"

"I don't think so. I'm sure something will come to mind during the day; if it does, I'll call you."

"I'll get back to it. Ring you if anything useful crops up."

"Good luck." Katy ended the call and blew out a breath. "If I wasn't confused before, I am now. What do you make of the situation, Charlie?"

She shrugged. "It's beyond me at the moment. Maybe it signifies that the attack was more of a personal nature than one of chance which could occur through a robbery. Or maybe I'm talking out of my arse and don't know what to think."

Katy laughed at the expression pulling at her features. "I'm glad it's not just me feeling discombobulated. There, I promised AJ I would drop that word into a conversation today and I've fulfilled my promise, or threat, should I say."

Charlie laughed. "I was about to ask if you'd swallowed a dictionary for breakfast instead of your cereal. Does this mean I have this sort of thing to contend with on a daily basis?"

Chuckling, Katy indicated and moved into a gap in the traffic. "I'll try not to torture you too much. It's a game we play at the weekends, it keeps our minds active."

Her partner glanced out of the window and mumbled something incoherent.

"I missed that, what did you say?"

"Whatever floats your boat."

"Enough said. Let's return to base, see what the rest of the team have managed to dig up on the family."

"I think that's a very wise move."

*K*aren had a snippet of news for them upon their arrival. "Boss, I've got the bank accounts for the victim and his daughter. Sadly, nothing to report there. Nadia was better off than her father by a mere few hundred pounds."

"Hardly ground-breaking news to help the investigation, no disrespect intended on your skills, Karen. We need more to go on than we've got so far. Looks like our only hope is that Patrick and Stephen have some form of success with the house-to-house task—that's likely to take a few hours yet."

"Sorry," Karen muttered.

Katy wagged her finger at the sergeant. "Don't you dare. If the clues aren't there then there's nothing we can do about it. I'll bring the board up to date, maybe my partner will feel sorry for me and buy me a coffee to battle my blues."

Charlie tutted and made her way over to the machine. "Anyone else want one while I'm here?"

Graham and Karen both raised their hands.

Katy smiled and scribbled on the whiteboard, noting down that the family photo was missing from the house, something, the more she thought about, the more she considered to be a significant fact. After she'd completed the task, she drifted into her office just as the phone rang. She raced around the desk to answer it. "DI Katy Foster, how can I help?"

"Hi, it's Sean. I've heard on the grapevine a new case has landed on your desk."

"Heard on the grapevine, have you? The jungle drums were correct."

"Do you want to run it past me?"

"Not really. So far there's not much to tell."

"Go on, I'm only sitting here twiddling my thumbs anyway." He sucked in a breath.

"Are you all right? You don't sound it."

"Fine. The stitches punishing me, that's all."

"You're nuts being back at work so soon. If I were in your shoes, I would have milked it for at least a couple of months."

Sean laughed. "And I'd call you a liar to your face. Don't give me that bullshit, you'd be back behind your desk within a week, knowing you."

"I wouldn't be so sure about that. I have a five-year-old who I'm barely seeing at the moment."

"Yeah, I have a child of similar age, so I totally hear you on that score."

"How did Sara take your injury?" Katy asked, referring to his daughter.

"She clucked around, fussed over me like a mother hen. I didn't get a lot of sympathy from Carmen."

"Should that surprise you, considering you're now divorced?"

"I guess. It would've been nice to know that she still cared a touch. No such luck. I suppose that's told me one thing: there's no way back, even if I had thoughts in that direction."

"Life goes on, Sean. It won't do you any good dwelling on what might have been. There are plenty more—"

"Please don't finish that shitty proverb. At my age, the last thing I need is to go to any nightclubs on a fishing expedition."

"Actually, I'd feel the same and I'm, what, a good ten years younger than you?"

"Cheeky sod."

"Have you thought about swiping right?"

"Thought about it, yes, done anything about it, no. I've figured it's not my scene. I'll be fine, don't worry about me, I'm feeling sorry for myself, that's all. Back to the case. Anything I can help you with?"

"Not really. You know what we're up against during the first few days of an investigation. This one is no different. To give you a brief rundown, Nadia Crawford, who is a nurse, came home from work to find her father sparked out on the floor with his throat cut."

"Heck, poor woman. Why aren't you treating it as a cut-and-dried case?"

"Because certain facts have come out."

"Are you going to share those with me or are you expecting me to guess what they are, Inspector?"

She disclosed the main points causing her concern.

"So, what you're really telling me is that because she was covered in his blood you think she has something to do with his death?"

"See, that's my dilemma. I do and I don't. On the one hand, I can understand why, as a nurse, she would want to try and help her father, but on the other, shouldn't she have known not to touch the body, or at least take a step back?"

"To me, instinct would and could have thrown all logic out of the window. My advice would be not to come down too heavily on her. She's grieving, you need to remember that."

"I know, which is why I've kept a rein on my doubts up until now. What about her father having cancer and her not knowing, what do you read into that?"

He sighed. "Not a lot. From a male point of view, we don't tend to take much notice of our health, or should I say, we prefer not to burden our loved ones with issues like that. Take me for instance. The doctor told me I shouldn't return to work for at least six months, and here I am, sitting behind my desk ready for action after only a week."

"Yeah, but you have a screw loose. Oops…sorry, did I say that out loud?" Katy laughed.

"You can mock me all you like, Katy Foster, or should that be Jackson? Either way, men react differently to women when they're injured or sick, we all know that."

"But cancer? You'd keep that illness from your loved ones?"

"I'm not sure I would have. Look, until you delve into the type of relationship they had, you can't really speculate, can you?"

"True enough. Father and daughter shared the same house, meaning they must have been close. The fact that she's a nurse and he kept the truth from her is becoming a thorn in my side. I simply can't get my head around it. Have you got any idea how much chemo takes out of the person being treated? She wasn't aware he was having it. I find that incredulous to believe."

"Are you sure she didn't know? You've only got the doctor's word on that, right?"

"True, I suppose. I really need to have another chat with her. There are too many variables I need to sort out."

"I don't have to tell you to be sensible about this, do I?"

"You're right, you don't. Otherwise, I would've hauled her arse in for questioning already."

"Okay, that's me told. Any issues, you know where I am. Try not tie yourself up in knots on this one, not yet anyway."

"Thanks for your support, sir," she replied, her words etched with sarcasm.

"You're welcome."

She ended the call, shaking her head. Two hours of mindless paperwork would sort her out.

Halfway through her mundane chore, Patrick called.

"Hi, how's it going down there?"

"I think we have something, boss. One of the elderly neighbours was taking his pooch for a walk and spotted someone in a hoodie lingering on the corner."

She sat upright and pulled her shoulders back. "Excellent news. Did he get a good look at them?"

"I wouldn't get too excited. Mr Cole told me he's as blind as a bat without his glasses on, and here's the bad news: he never ventures out with his glasses on, doesn't see the point in wearing them out in the street at night."

"What the actual fuck is that supposed to mean? Jesus, some people's ideas get skewed as they get older, don't they? Okay, is that all?"

"Yes, at the moment."

"Well, keep knocking on the doors. If one person saw a stranger lurking, the odds are in our favour that someone else might have seen them, too. Good job, Patrick."

"Thanks for the unexpected praise, boss, I wouldn't get too carried away just yet. Back to the grind. I'll call you if anything else shows up."

Katy hung up and glanced up at the blue skies taunting her through the window. What she wouldn't give to be sunbathing on a Greek island instead of being stuck inside on one of the hottest days of the year. She jumped up and opened the window a bit wider, her mind in desperate need of a break.

Charlie knocked on her door and entered. "Just checking to see if you're surviving okay."

"I am, thanks. Patrick just called. One of the neighbours spotted someone on the street corner."

"Interesting. Is that it?"

"Yep, the neighbour has notoriously bad eyesight."

"Helpful." Charlie rolled her eyes.

"Not really. Patrick is surging on, in the hope that another neighbour witnessed the same person. I hope it doesn't turn out to be a wild goose chase or the equivalent. I don't think my nerves could stand it."

"We're plodding on with the background checks and getting nowhere fast."

"We need a break. Do you think the perp knew the victim was dying?"

"We have no way of knowing that. What's your line of thinking there, that someone might have set out to have intentionally done him a favour?"

Katy's arms flew out to the sides then slammed against her thighs. "Who bloody knows? At this juncture, I'm willing to listen to every plausible option going. Let's face it, we're paddling against the tide so far."

"True enough. I wouldn't know where to begin if you asked me to take a punt on my suggestion."

"Nope, me neither. We'll bear it in mind and move on." She clicked her fingers. "Patrick also informed me that when Nadia showed up at the house, she requested a family photo from the lounge. The frame was empty; she was distraught about that."

"It doesn't make sense. If we're putting this down to a burglary, I've never heard of a burglar taking a photo out of a frame and leaving with the picture, have you?"

"Never. Perplexing ain't the word, is it?"

"It's all beyond me. I don't mind admitting that I'm out of my depth on this one, sorry."

"Bollocks, don't you dare apologise. We're all out of our depths, Charlie. Until more clues or evidence comes our way then we're screwed, well and truly."

"I forgot the evidence part. Maybe they'll find a fingerprint on the frame."

"Possibly." She ran a finger and thumb around her chin as she thought. "I know one thing, this case is doing my head in already, and we're less than twenty-four hours into it."

"Maybe we're guilty of overthinking things because of the way Nadia dealt with her father at the scene."

"I think you're right. I need to block that from my mind until some form of evidence pointing in her direction shows up. If we're going along the lines of a simple burglary, we need to find out how the bastard got in."

"Maybe Bruce Crawford let the intruder in," Charlie said with a shrug.

"As in, the person walked up to the front door and knocked on it?"

Charlie chuckled. "Now you've said it out loud, perhaps that was a daft suggestion. Proves I'm struggling as much as you are."

Katy stretched her arms up over her head and yawned. "It's draining the shit out of me. I'm going to give the hotel where Nadia is staying a call. Her sister should have arrived by now, right?"

Charlie nodded. "I think so. Want me to do it for you?"

"Go on then. I could do with emptying my bladder. I'll be right back."

"TMI," Charlie grumbled and turned her back.

Katy rushed past her, in a hurry to go to the loo now she'd mentioned it. She tidied up her hair while she was in the ladies' and, after spending a penny and washing her hands, returned to the incident room. She was greeted by a smiling Charlie, her puzzling frown a thing of the past. "I take it you've got some good news for a change."

"Yep, she's not long arrived. I asked the receptionist to put me through to her room. She's willing to meet up with us. I told her to expect us within half an hour. She'll be waiting for us in the bar."

"What are we waiting for then? Let's get going. We'll pick up a sandwich on the way. Anyone else want one?"

"I could do with a cheese and pickle on white, boss, and a sneaky doughnut on the side." Graham dug into his pocket and withdrew his wallet.

Katy held up a hand. "I'll get them, I'm feeling generous."

"I won't argue with you then." Graham grinned.

"Karen?"

"Thanks all the same, boss, but I knocked up a salad before I came to work. It's sitting in the fridge."

Katy winked. "Rather you than me. I don't know how you find the time to prepare anything first thing."

"Where there's a will… I've got a wedding coming up at the end of the month, I need to fit into my dress, otherwise I'll have to buy another one, and funds are tight right now."

"Great incentive. Charlie, are you ready?"

"Ready when you are."

They left the station and stopped off at the baker's a few streets away. "What do you fancy?" Katy asked, ready to dart into the shop.

"Tuna and mayo on a brown roll, if you don't mind. I'll skip the afters, though."

"I think I'll have the same. I won't be a jiffy."

*A*fter eating their lunch and swilling it down with the water Katy had bought, taking a leaf out of Charlie's well-intention book, they made their way inside the hotel to the bar area. Charlie was the first to spot Penny. She was sitting at the table in front of the bay window staring at the passersby in the street.

"Hi, would you be Penny?" Katy asked.

"Sorry, I was miles away. Wishing I was back up in Scotland with my hubby. Yes. Are you the detective I spoke to earlier?"

Katy and Charlie flashed their warrant cards.

"My partner did. DI Katy Foster and DC Charlie Simpkins. Thank you for agreeing to see us, we're so sorry for your loss."

Tears sparkled in the young woman's eyes. She motioned for them to take a seat and then sipped at her coffee. "Can I get you a drink?"

"No, thank you, we've not long had one. Did you have a good trip down?"

"Long and boring. I hate train journeys at the best of times. Sitting there contemplating what I've been told about my father's death… well, it made the journey a thousand times worse."

"I can imagine. Will you be here long?"

"I'll be around however long my sister needs me. I can't believe she's decided to continue to work. If I'd known she wouldn't be around, I think I would've stayed at home and travelled down just to attend the funeral. Do you know when that's likely to be?"

Katy shook her head. "I don't think the pathologist will delay releasing your father's body. It'll be up to you and Nadia to make the arrangements then. Could be a few weeks or months, depending how busy the funeral home is."

"I can't face it. I think Nadia has it all in hand, at least, that's what she told me."

"I see. She seems a very level-headed person to me."

"You're not wrong. She was always more practical than me. I have a tendency to fall apart at the seams when faced with adverse circumstances such as this."

"Are you up to speaking to us today? The last thing I want to do is cause you any further distress, especially after your long journey."

"Of course. Don't worry about me. I must warn you I'm still a bit tearful and I might break down and cry now and again, so you'll have to forgive me if that happens."

"Don't worry about it. You do what you have to do to cope with your grief. Were you close to your father?"

"Sort of. Not as close as my sister has been over the years. We… how can I put this? I suppose tolerated each other, would be the truth."

"I see. Any specific reason for the relationship being strained?"

"I couldn't tell you. I think Nadia has always been more of a daddy's girl than me."

"I have to ask you something and I'm not sure how you're going to react."

Her cornflower-blue eyes widened in anticipation. "Sounds ominous. Go for it."

"Were you aware that your father only had a few weeks or months to live?"

She gasped. Fresh tears seeped into her eyes, and she shook her head. "No. Bloody hell, did my sister know?"

"According to your father's doctor, no. Although we intend chasing that up, when we get the chance."

"What was it?"

"Stomach cancer. Why do you think your father chose to keep it a secret from you and Nadia?"

"I don't know. How awful. You'd think he would tell us as we're his only surviving relatives, wouldn't you?"

"It's hard for us to fathom out why he wouldn't want his children to know, especially as he'd gone through chemo as well."

"What? I can't believe what you're telling me. Wouldn't my sister have known, what with her working at the hospital?"

"We need to run our findings past Nadia. I didn't want to disrupt her shift today."

She shook her head again. "I can't figure this out. Why wouldn't Nadia know about this? Dad would've had medicine to take, wouldn't he? She lives with him, wouldn't she have spotted him popping some pills? Did she care that little about him?"

Katy inclined her head and asked, "What makes you say that? Have they fallen out recently?"

Penny ran a shaking hand over her face and into her hair. "I don't know. You'll have to ask her."

Katy had a suspicion that Penny knew more than she was letting on but chose not to push her on the subject. "I'm sorry if this has come as a shock to you."

"Why didn't he tell us? Didn't he love us? He couldn't have done, right? Not to keep us in the dark like that. He just couldn't have. Oh God, here I go again." She searched her handbag, sitting on the seat next to her, and extracted a tissue. "I'm at a loss. I'm confused and bewildered. Maybe I'm more tired than I thought after my journey. I don't think I can blame it all on that, though."

"Please, try not to upset yourself. Your father must've had a good reason to keep his illness from you. He didn't want to burden you both."

"But he was my *father*, fathers aren't supposed to do that, are they?"

"Men can be stubborn fools at times. Maybe he thought the chemo was going to make him better."

"I don't know. I'm struggling to make any sense of it. Nadia said that someone must've entered our house but she had a quick look around and couldn't see any signs of a break-in. Why? There should've been. It's not like Dad would've opened the door and let a stranger in at that time of night. I don't think he would have anyway."

"We're still waiting on the report from the Scenes of Crimes Officers who are currently examining the house."

"Let's hope they find something to help you guys."

"It's rare for a criminal not to leave some form of clue behind. Maybe you can cast your mind back a few months. Over that time, has your father intimated that anything might have been wrong at home? I'm not referring to the cancer, I mean life in general. He'd possibly fallen out with someone."

She shook her head slowly. "No, you're asking the wrong sister. Nadia would be the one to give you a definite answer there. You think someone he knew did this to him, is that what you're saying in a roundabout way?"

"Possibly. I can't go into detail, I wouldn't want to upset you more than you are now, but the way your father was killed, well, the pathologist has suggested that might be the case."

Her eyes widened at the revelation. "Jesus, is that true? I find that hard to believe."

"May I ask why?"

"I don't know, maybe I felt that was the right thing to say. Perhaps I didn't really know my father after all. You should be asking my sister all this. She'd be able to tell you like that." She clicked her finger and thumb together.

"Maybe if your sister hadn't chosen to go back to work so soon, we would have been able to."

"Don't ask. I haven't got a clue why she insisted continuing to work. Surely her employers would understand. We're talking about the NHS here, for God's sake. She needs this time to grieve, we both do. I could do with her support right now. I know that and I didn't even really know the man, not as well as she did. Sorry, I'm rambling."

Katy smiled. "You're doing fine. Your sister told us that your mother died when you were both very young. Does that mean your father brought both of you up on his own or did he have another girl-friend after your mother left? Or possibly a second wife?"

Her head bent low. "I don't remember my mother. I think I was three when she died. Nadia says she remembers her a little, but not that much. And no, our father has never had a regular woman in his life since she died."

"No one regular but the odd girlfriend, I take it?"

Penny sighed. "I think I can recall him having a few…liaisons, shall we call them. Drunken nights of sex with the odd woman. Nadia and I used to sleep in the same bed, huddled to each other when the women started screaming. At the time, we thought he was hurting them. Of course, we know better now and acknowledge that it was… I'm sure I don't need to go into detail, you're not silly, you can figure that part out for yourselves, can't you?"

"I understand what you're saying. And none of these women stuck around for more than a few days, or nights, should I say?"

"They might have done. They showed up after the pub and left before we got up the next day. Nadia and I always remained in our bedroom until he gave us permission to leave it. When we came down for breakfast, the women had usually gone."

"I see. Do you remember this happening often?"

"No, not really. Gosh, don't ask me to think back, I've blocked out so many things from my childhood…"

Katy inclined her head. "Meaning it was bad for you?"

Penny swallowed and covered her eyes with her hands. Her shoulders jiggled. Katy glanced at Charlie and grimaced, then looked back at Penny who was clearly upset.

"I'm sorry. I can't talk about it. I've locked most of it away in the box at the back of my mind. I don't want to go back there. Please, please, don't force me to relive the…"

"I'm sorry, Penny, I'm not forcing you to do anything. However, if there's something we should know, it would be better for you to be open with us."

Her hand dropped to reveal yet more tears. "It's hard. I can't go through that again."

"Go through what? Are you telling us that your father…abused you?"

Penny gasped and glanced around her to see if anyone had overheard what Katy had said. "I can't say for sure. I've truly blocked my childhood out. Something happened when I was small, and I can't for the life of me tell you what it was. I used to be very withdrawn as a child, saw several psychiatrists and counsellors throughout my formative years. Maybe that's bullshit, about the psychiatrists, I mean, they came later in life. I know I was forced to see a few counsellors when I was at school."

"I'm sorry to hear that. Do you think your mother's death hit you harder than it affected Nadia? Did she go through the same tussle as a child?"

"No, I don't think she ever melted down, not like I did."

"Do you remember why you had the meltdown? What specific incident led to it?"

She shook her head. "No, not now, maybe in time it will come to me."

"What age did you leave the family home?"

"On my sixteenth birthday. I ran away to make my own life in this world. It was foolish of me, I realise that now, but at the time I thought it was the only option open to me."

"Did Nadia try to dissuade you?" Katy asked, her heart full of sadness for the woman sitting in front of her.

"Yes, I put the plan into action months before. I tried to make her see sense and pleaded with her to come with me. She refused to leave him, said it would destroy him if we both left. I wasn't prepared to stick around…"

"And be abused," Katy finished off for her.

"Yes. I lived on the streets for a few years until I eventually got my shit together and found my husband. We've been married for five years, and I couldn't be happier. A vast contrast to the time I spent with my father, the only other dominant male in my life thus far."

"You had no other family members around you as you were growing up?"

"No. If there were any, they never visited the house. Maybe that was their choice. I fear it was more at my father's request. He insisted he didn't need anyone else, as long as he had his daughters around him and the odd whore to screw now and again."

"Whore? Are you telling us these women were likely sex workers?"

Her shoulders nudged upwards. "I don't know. I just presumed they were because they popped up out of nowhere and then disappeared, never to be seen a second time. Not that we ever met them, of course. I'm sorry, I'm not making any sense."

"I think I understand what you're saying. They were one-night stands, most of them, right?"

"Correct."

"I'm sorry to have to press you, but can you tell us what form the abuse was?"

Penny paused, fidgeted in her seat for several moments, and then heaved out a sigh. "Like I say, I think I've blocked that side of my life out. All I know is that my existence with him was fraught and filled with unhappiness, that's all I can tell you."

"It's okay. The last thing I want you to feel is uncomfortable answering my questions. Let's leave it there for now. Will you be okay?"

"I think so. I'll ring Andy in a moment, he understands me better than anyone. Always manages to say the right thing at the right time.

I'm a different person to the one who used to live around here, that's for sure."

"And yet you've always remained close to Nadia, is that right?"

"Yes, we found a way of staying in contact with each other throughout our lives."

"Did your father know she was in contact with you?"

"I think deep down he did. I don't think he had the courage to tackle her about the situation, though."

"Did your father ever try to get in touch with you?"

"No. As far as I was concerned, I was dead to him the second I walked out on him and Nadia."

"Sorry to hear that, and yet here you are, why?"

"I'm here to offer my sister the support she deserves. She needs me, although by her decision to continue working, that clearly isn't true. I'll see when the funeral is and make my way home again. I hate this area, always have done. Scotland is where my heart lies, now more than ever."

"Some places draw us more than others, I get that."

"So true. Will that be all?"

"I think so. I'll leave you my card. If you think of anything else that might help us solve your father's case, please ring me."

"I will. I'm sorry for divulging what I did. I've struggled with my feelings towards that man for most of my life. Maybe it was the relief of knowing that he has finally gone that gave me the courage to open up after all these years."

"Maybe. I'm glad you did. It sheds a different light on what type of man he was and the likelihood of his murderer being known to him in spite of what your sister tells us. One last question, if I may? Did your father work and, if so, where?"

"Nadia mentioned something about him working at a sawmill a few years ago. I don't know if he was still there, especially if he'd been ill lately. Again, you'd be better off asking her about that."

"Thanks. Take care of yourself. I'm sorry if talking to us has brought back memories you'd rather have kept buried."

"Thank you. I'm sure I'll be fine once the funeral is out of the way."

Katy reached out and shook the woman's hand. "Our paths might cross again soon, if you're sticking around for a few days."

"No doubt. I hope you find the person who killed him."

"We're going to do our very best."

Katy and Charlie left the hotel and returned to the car. Katy checked her phone to find she had a missed call because she'd put it on silent, not wishing to be disturbed.

She dialled Patrick's number. "Hi, sorry, I was interviewing some-one. What have you got, anything?"

"An extra sighting, boss."

"Go on."

"One of the neighbours opposite the Crawfords' house spotted the hooded person coming out of the front door. They ran down a nearby alleyway."

"What time was this, Patrick?"

"He was putting the kettle on and thinks it was around ten-fifteen but then he said it might have been five or ten minutes later, so strug-gled to give a definitive time."

"So a fifteen-minute window. That sounds good to me. I think Nadia said she arrived home around ten-twenty, which means she only just missed bumping into the attacker. Any further description of the person?"

"Slight build, he thinks, and some form of athlete by the speed he took off at, according to the neighbour."

"Okay, it's not much but it's more than we had. Get a statement from him, Patrick, and then if you've spoken to everyone you can possibly speak to, return to the station. We're on our way back there now."

"We'll do that, boss. See you later."

Katy ended the call and stared out of the windscreen for a few seconds, collecting her thoughts. "Well, that sounds promising, doesn't it?"

"Which part?" Charlie asked. "The witness seeing a person leaving the house or were you referring to what Penny just divulged back there?"

"I suppose both. I must say, what Penny told us made my skin crawl. What about you?"

"We don't know what we've got until it's too late. Some folks should treat their parents better in my eyes, because there will always be others out there who've had a rough childhood and gone through major trauma at the hands of a parent."

"That's so true. Hearing what those girls went through definitely puts your own life into perspective. Here's what's bugging me about Nadia: if what Penny told us is true, that they were both abused by the father, then why, oh why, did Nadia stick around and not leave like her sister, or even with her?"

"Pass. I've been asking myself the very same question since Penny first raised the subject. It's disgusting, the way he treated his kids. You have to wonder if he'd have done the same had his wife not died."

"Exactly. Maybe her dying and leaving him to care for his daughters alone triggered something within him. I don't know, I'm just throwing that out there, seeing if it sticks. One thing's for sure, this case is getting more and more complex the more we dig."

"It is that. What about Nadia and her reluctance to take time off? That kind of makes sense now, doesn't it?"

"It does, although I'd rather get the facts from her own mouth than speculate about it."

3

_____

 early a week later, and the investigation was no further forward, not really. Yes, they had the two sightings of the person in the hoodie, but that was where that lead started and ended, much to the team's frustration.

This was the day of the funeral. Katy hadn't attended many attached to a case before, just the odd few with her previous partner when the investigation appeared to be stuck in the doldrums. She'd insisted that Charlie dress in suitable attire, and here they were, parked up outside St Anne's Church, both swathed in black, waiting for the hearse to arrive.

"Not the best day to have one, judging by the darkening clouds overhead," Katy admitted.

"Have you ever been to one when it hasn't poured down with rain? I don't think I have."

Katy cast her mind back. "Thinking about it, no, I don't believe I have. Come on, let's join the gathering mourners. I have to say, I'm blown away by the number of people here."

"Former work colleagues perhaps?"

"Yep. I suppose when we visited the firm last week, they had more staff working there than I had anticipated. There's Nadia and Penny.

Let's go and have a quick word with them before anyone else pounces on them."

They left the vehicle and headed towards the two women. Penny smiled. She appeared to be taking the day in her stride. Nadia was busy scanning the crowd when they stopped next to her.

"Hi, Penny and Nadia. We hope you don't mind us being here today?"

Penny shook her head. "Glad you could make it. Any news, or is this the wrong time to ask?"

"Yes, it is," Nadia jumped in before Katy had the chance to respond.

"We can discuss the investigation later, at your leisure, Nadia, that's no problem," Katy suggested, giving the grieving woman the benefit of the doubt. "It's a good turnout for your father. Are these all his colleagues from work?"

"A mixture of friends and colleagues. I went through his address book. I'm as surprised as you to see how many have shown up," Nadia informed them.

"A popular man by all accounts," Katy added, if only to see the sisters' reactions.

Penny rolled her eyes and glanced over her shoulder at the crowd gathered behind her. "I suppose so," she replied, a note of bitterness in her tone.

"Not today, Penny," Nadia warned.

"What did I say? Don't start on me, Nadia, I've had it with you and your bloody bossy attitude the last few days. I needn't have come back down for this…this…farce of a funeral."

Katy was tempted to step in to calm the situation down, but any copper worth their salt opened their ears and shut their mouths when an argument kicked off. It was always a surprise to hear what ended up being revealed in anger.

"I wish you'd stayed away, if that's your attitude. It's not like you loved him at all, is it?"

Penny's jaw dropped. She recovered within a few seconds and leaned in to her sister. "And we both know why that is, don't we? When are you going to realise what a bastard he was, Nadia?"

"Stop it! Not here, not when we're about to bury the poor man."

"Poor man! You're having a sodding laugh." Penny's voice had risen, attracting the attention of the crowd.

"Maybe you should both calm down a bit. Leave this discussion until the service has ended," Katy finally interjected.

Both sisters glared at her interference. Katy smiled, trying to deflect the irate glares Penny and Nadia were directing at her.

Finally, Penny sighed. "She's right. This conversation can wait. We'd better get inside, the vicar is waiting for us."

Katy glanced at the church doorway to find a young vicar welcoming the mourners into his domain.

"Don't think this is the end of it, Penny," Nadia snapped through gritted teeth.

Katy and Charlie held back so the others could get seated first.

Katy turned her back on the mourners and whispered, "They both seem on edge. We'll keep a close eye on them during the service."

Charlie nodded. "Should we try and sit closer to them, in order for us to do that?"

"No, I think we'll be better off sitting at the rear. That way we can oversee everything that is happening in front of us."

"Good idea."

"Come on, it's time for us to go in before they carry the coffin in."

They chose to sit on the right-hand side, in the final pew. There were several pews empty ahead of them, but Katy stuck to her decision to sit at the back and observe.

The music started up, and four pallbearers carried the coffin down the aisle and settled it on a couple of trestles near the altar. The vicar was very complimentary about the victim during his service. Katy kept a close eye on Penny and Nadia throughout. Penny remained upright, but Nadia held her head low at all times. There were a few eulogies read, one by a work colleague—actually, it was Crawford's boss who took up the role. The second one was read out by Nadia. Throughout the reading she came across as a sincere and loving daughter. Katy noticed the way Penny shook her head constantly during her sister's speech.

But it was after the service that things really became interesting. The same four men carried the coffin out to its final resting place. The hole had been dug, and the coffin was lowered into the ground. Penny and Nadia stood next to each other, a few feet apart, acting like strangers rather than siblings. For some reason this upset Katy. The sisters should be supporting each other not falling out, bickering.

Katy and Charlie stood opposite the sisters and scanned the crowd at regular intervals. Most of the mourners were men, with the exception of a few women dotted around here and there. Katy couldn't help wondering if some of the women were the ones Penny had referred to, who had once upon a time shared their father's bed, if only for the night.

The pallbearers seemed to be gathered in one area, all appearing to be the same age, similar to that of Bruce Crawford, which made Katy wonder if they'd been lifelong chums and even gone to school with one another. Maybe she should interview them afterwards.

"How are you holding up?" Katy whispered to Charlie.

"Bored out of my mind but doing fine, you?"

"The same. Keep vigilant, you never know. One of those present here today could be our killer. It's not unheard of for the guilty party to attend the funeral, it's happened in a few of the cases I've dealt with over the years."

"Hard to believe. I'll keep an eye open."

Katy's attention returned to studying the sisters. Nadia went from having her chin settled on her chest to surveying the crowd. Now and then, Katy spotted her eyes narrowing a little and couldn't help wondering why. As usual, she had the feeling there was more to this woman than met the eye. She just couldn't figure out what it could be. Was she the killer? Had she left the hospital that night, worn a disguise, done the deed, and then run back to her car and pretended to arrive home to find her father still breathing? The more that scenario raced through her head, the more she thought it conceivable—or was it? She had conflicting ideas. One second she thought she was doing the nurse an injustice, the next she had her nailed as the bloody killer who had, up until now, smartly covered her tracks.

Once the vicar invited the mourners to throw soil or a flower onto the coffin and say a few words to send Crawford's spirit on its way, the two sisters stood together to say farewell to those who had shown up and thank them for attending.

"I take it there's not going to be a wake," Charlie said out of the corner of her mouth.

"So it would appear. I suppose the cost would come into it, and if Penny has dug her heels in, it would be left up to Nadia to meet those costs. No idea how she afforded this when she said she didn't have any money, you know, at the beginning when we were discussing her moving into a hotel for a few days."

"She did. Fair enough. What next?"

"We wait until everyone has gone. Maybe we should split up, listen to a couple of the conversations, see if we glean anything from them."

"I'm up for it." Charlie set off.

Katy stepped closer to the sisters who were shaking hands with an elderly man and his wife.

"So very sorry for your loss, girls. Your father will be missed terribly at work, he was well-liked, as you can see from the turnout you've had today. We closed the firm for the day to allow the whole workforce to pay their respects."

"Thanks for coming." Nadia smiled tightly at the man. "It must have come as a shock to you and your colleagues. Did you know he wasn't well?"

The man's brow furrowed. "No, no I didn't."

Nadia nodded. "Neither did we, he kept the cancer from us."

"Cancer? Oh my goodness, surely not."

"It's true. He'd even had chemo and didn't tell us."

"But you're a nurse, aren't you, dear?" the man's wife asked.

"Yes. I don't know what he was thinking. Maybe he thought he was indestructible and didn't want to burden us. It was a shock when the police made us aware of the situation."

"I can only imagine what you poor girls went through," the man's wife said, seeming genuinely upset by the news.

"It is what it is. At the end of the day, I think it's proved what a complex person our father was. To have held on to a secret as great as that and neither of us recognising the change in him."

"I wouldn't have known either way, living in Scotland," Penny piped up.

Nadia chose to ignore her sister's input into the conversation. Penny kicked out at a stone at her feet, appearing to suppress the anger bubbling inside her.

Katy stepped closer as the queue grew smaller. The pallbearers were next. One by one, they apologised to the girls for not being there when they needed them the most, or when their father had needed them in recent years.

Nadia nodded but kept her mouth shut, and Penny did the same. The air surrounding them was one of extreme awkwardness. The men hurried past and gathered in the car park. Four men, no female company, all appearing to be uncomfortable in their surroundings.

Katy held her hand out to shake Nadia's and then Penny's. "Thank you for allowing us to attend today. I'm sorry we haven't got any positive news to share with you regarding your father's case. I put out an appeal to the general public a few days ago, but we've been disappointed by the lack of information we've received to date."

"It is what it is. I'm sure you're doing your best, Inspector," Penny replied.

Nadia remained quiet, lost in thought.

"I hope to be in touch with some good news soon," Katy responded.

"Keep us informed," Nadia said, her tone flat and dismissive.

"Of course we will." Katy held the woman's gaze for a while before moving on.

She and Charlie marched back to the car, slowing down as they got closer to the pallbearers who were all looking their way for some reason.

"That was strange, wasn't it?" Charlie noted once they were back in the car.

"Yep, it has to be up there for awkward moment of the century, I'll grant you that. I'm getting the distinct impression there's still more to this case than meets the eye but I'll be buggered if I know what. I was hoping running the appeal would flood us with clues to chase up. It didn't. So where the fuck do we go now?" She turned the engine over and drove out of the church's car park ahead of the rest of the cars.

"You sound defeated."

"Truthfully? I feel it. I hate the fact a man has lost his life and no one is behind bars yet. That can't be right, can it?"

"I know, but if the clues or evidence aren't there, what do you suggest we do, plant it?"

Katy twisted her head sharply towards her partner. "I would never do that, Charlie, and I'm mortified that you would suggest such a despicable thing."

"Sorry, it came out wrong...or maybe it didn't. Oh, I don't know. I suppose I'm just as frustrated about this investigation as you are. Does this type of thing happen often?"

Katy smiled, accepting her apology. "Once in a blue moon. All cases can have levels of frustration thrown into the mix, I guess. But to have nothing after a week is beyond me. We've done as much digging as we possibly can. I'm surprised Karen isn't speaking to us from a station in Australia by now."

"You can imagine it, can't you? Her sitting at a desk in the Outback somewhere, having a conversation with a gathering of kangaroos trying to get something out of them."

"That does summon up a hilarious image. Talking of which, do you know the correct term for a group of kangas?"

"Is there one? I've never really thought about it before. Go on, don't tell me this is another one of your off-the-wall facts you're going to fling at me?"

"It is. Get this, it's either a mob, troop or court of kangaroos. Can you believe the last one? You've heard of a kangaroo court before, right?"

"Yeah, of course I have. Seems bizarre to be connected."

"That's what I thought. Anyway, I thought I'd brighten your day with that little gem, I only learnt about it last week."

"I bet you never thought that fact would see the light of day, eh?"

They both laughed, relieving the tension that had descended.

4

———

"We'll see you later, Dale. Have a good evening."

"Thanks, the wife and I are visiting friends tonight for a catch-up. See you tomorrow." Dale waved at the group of teacher colleagues and climbed into his car. He drove through the country lanes back to his cottage on autopilot, mulling over some of the lessons he'd given during the day, mostly furious by the lack of response to his questions from his students. What he wouldn't give for a group of youngsters craving to learn more, eager to bombard him with questions, no matter how trivial or mundane they sounded, and yet he got nothing. The students of today just weren't the same as they had once been in the past.

Leading him to wonder at times whether his own standards had slipped. Or was their lack of response due to them being deficient in any form of interest in learning full stop? He feared it was the latter and prayed it wasn't the former. If that ever happened, he'd chuck in the towel and retire immediately. *Now that's a thought! At fifty-five, could I?* He vowed to speak to his good friend, Simon, who was also his financial advisor, to run the idea past him. But then, raising that subject in his mind led him off in a different direction. Could he bear to stay at home all day with Adele, his wife of twenty-five years?

His attention was drawn to a car travelling behind him. It was closer than he felt comfortable with. Maybe up the road he'd pull over to allow the vehicle to pass. The driver was clearly in a hurry. Around the next bend, he slowed down and indicated. He turned into the next available road and let the car pass. The movement went without a hitch, no angry blast on the horn from the driver, nothing.

He continued on his journey. His house was only a couple of miles away. Time to ring Adele, tell her he was not too far from home. That way she'd have a nice cold beer waiting for him for when he walked through the back door.

Another sharp bend up ahead. He pressed his foot gently on the brake and eased around the curve. "What the...bloody idiot, what in God's name is he doing standing there like that?"

He slammed the brakes on and drew the car to a halt. In front of him, the driver who had not long passed him had angled his car across the lane, effectively blocking all traffic from both directions.

Dale opened his car door and got out. He leaned on the top. "What's the meaning of this? Kindly move your vehicle so I can get past. I have a very important meeting I have to attend this evening, and you're holding me up."

The figure refused to move an inch. Arms folded, leaning against the bonnet.

"Hey, you, did you hear me? Are you deaf or something? Move your damn car. Now."

Again, the driver didn't respond. By this time, Dale was beginning to get a stirring in his stomach, signifying that something was wrong. He cast an eye over his shoulder, pondered whether he had it in him to reverse all the way back to the road he'd pulled in for this person to pass him.

When he turned back to face the person, he found them standing within a foot of him. The stranger was dressed in a hoodie, their features masked by the excess fabric shielding their face.

Fear knotted his intestines. He really wasn't one for confrontation of any kind, even in the classroom with his students. Was this one of them? Were they doing this to get their kicks?

Instead of speaking, the stranger took two steps forward. They were barely six inches away now. Dale was glad the door was between them. His inquisitive nature got the better of him. He peered into the darkness of the fabric to try to see who the devil was haunting him like this. It proved to be a pointless task.

"You've had your fun, now let me pass if you will?"

The stranger shook their head and withdrew a long implement from their pocket. Making out what the item was, Dale backed away from the car. The driver remained where they were, adding to his trepidation.

What the hell does this individual want from me? Should I ask them or should I just run and take my chances that I'll outrun them? Although, I'm not as fit as I used to be, and they seem pretty agile to me. Shit! What do I do? Someone give me a sign, telling me what to do, for God's sake.

He attempted to get a conversation going between them again. "Please, I don't want any trouble. Is there something I can do for you?"

A growl left the stranger's mouth, and they stepped around the door and into his personal space once more. "You can die," came the person's sinister response.

"Wha...t? You can't mean that? I can't die now, I'm too young. We can work this out, if only you'd tell me what you want."

"Die! Die! Die!"

That one word was enough for Dale to want to take off. Fearing he wouldn't have enough time to get in his car and turn it around, he turned and hot-footed it down the lane, trying to think of a shortcut he could take across the fields to get to his house which was within spitting distance of where he was.

No, I'll be better off sticking to the main road. At least there's a chance of someone driving past.

Footsteps behind him. Petrified, he refused to peer over his shoulder, his fear forcing his legs to work. His mind whirred with horrendous ways in which the stranger could hurt him.

Die! I don't want to die. I have too much to live for. Adele and my five kids need me. I don't want to die. Please, don't let me die!

A pain erupted in his shoulder. "What the…? No, please, don't do this."

Yet another strike from his pursuant; this time the implement hit his right arm. He didn't cry out, as much as he wanted to. He refused to give the stranger the satisfaction of knowing they'd hurt him. No, he carried on running, his breath catching in his throat every time the assailant struck. Another stab, this time in his back. With each strike, his legs grew weaker. He stumbled as his foot slithered into a pothole. He'd tried to avoid it, but his vision had blurred and failed him at the last minute.

Shit! I don't have it in me to continue. I'm going to die! They're relentless, I can't make them stop. I have to make them see what they're doing is wrong, but how?

He stopped running and held his hands out in front of him to ward off any further attack. It was futile. The person ran at him, yelled out and stabbed his upper body over and over with the ice pick. Intense pain ripped through his body. Dale's legs buckled. He shook his head and stared up at the attacker standing over him.

"Please, tell me what I've done to deserve this?"

Instead of replying, the aggressor raised their arm and pounded the implement into his chest, over and over, each stab sending a searing heat through his upper torso.

"Don't do this. I have five kids. Adele and the kids rely on me. Without me, they won't survive. Think about it, please, I'm too young to die."

The assailant's arm raised above their head and, in what appeared to be slow motion, the ice pick came towards his face. He grappled behind him, searching for some kind of rock to use as a weapon, but there was nothing within reach. He used his arms to pull his body along the road, his legs weakly pushing him. He stared down at his chest, his white shirt stained with deep-red patches. He was doomed. He might as well give up, his strength was virtually non-existent now. His arms gave way beneath him. Crushed, he lay on the ground and stared up. His breath allowed one more attempt to save his life.

"Please, I'm begging you to spare me. I have money tucked away, you can have it all. It's supposed to be my retirement fund, but you can have it, all of it."

The stranger's arm rose again. The ice pick found its target. Dale cried out; the pick stuck in his throat. The assailant twisted the implement to make the hole wider, deeper. Dale had lost too much blood to continue his fight now. Instead, he made peace with his maker in his final few seconds, offering up a silent prayer. His eyes closed, blocking out the stranger at last, and he exhaled his final breath.

5

*K*aty received the call during the drive home that evening. She punched herself in the leg—she'd been looking forward to bathing Georgie and reading her a bedtime story. Instead, here she was, turning around and heading out to what appeared to be a murder scene. As if she didn't have enough on her plate already. Actually, that wasn't quite true. The Crawford case had ground to a halt, leading her to tell the desk sergeant to contact her if any other major crimes cropped up in the area.

"Charlie, did you get the call?" she asked through her hands-free.

"I did. I'm ten minutes out. Where are you?"

"I'm about the same, give or take. It's a gruesome one, so Mick said. Just what we need at this time of the day. Will Brandon be all right about you doing overtime if it's necessary?"

Charlie laughed. "You worry too much. He's a pussycat. I didn't give him the chance to complain. I've told you before, I'm committed to the job, Katy, there's no need to be concerned for me or my relationship."

"I'm not. Hey, forget I asked. I'll see you soon."

Katy ended the call and put her foot down. She arrived at the location soon after, Charlie not far behind her. They slipped on their protective suits and shoes and joined Patti on the other side of the cordon.

"What have we got?" Katy asked, staring down at the bloody mess lying horizontal on the tarmac.

"Looks like a murder scene to me. I know, stating the obvious as usual. You shouldn't ask such a stupid question," Patti said, a grin forming at the end of her tetchy response.

"Ha bloody ha. You definitely missed your vocation, Patti. You should have been a court jester."

"Cheek, do they even exist nowadays? For your information, I'm not that old, I'm considered to be in the prime of my life."

"At least you still have a life, unlike this chap. Bloody hell, someone really did a number on him, didn't they?"

"Oh God, I don't think I've ever seen something so horrendous. I'm having trouble holding on to my stomach here. I never thought I'd hear myself say that," Charlie piped up, a green tinge shadowing her features.

"Step away from my crime scene if you think you're going to spill your guts," Patti advised with a stern warning edging her tone.

"You do look a little off-colour. Go on, Charlie, step back. Either that or don't look at the victim."

"I can't help it, it's gross but compelling at the same time. I'm sure I'll be fine."

Katy and Patti rolled their eyes at each other.

"Anyway, my guys have had a chance to survey the area," Patti said. "Fifty yards or so up the road we have a hefty amount of blood spatter, telling us that in all probability the attack began back there and ended in the man's death here."

"Do you think someone did this to him…? I mean, yes, I appreciate someone killed him, but the eyes, do you think the perp did that or could it possibly be the birds treating him as roadkill and instantly going for his eyes?"

Patti stared at her. "Since when does a bird pluck out the eyes and leave them at the scene? You did notice them sitting on the man's chest, didn't you?"

"Sorry, my mistake. Okay, I should have realised what I was thinking was daft before saying it out loud."

"You're not wrong there. This was a hate crime. People rarely tend to inflict this much pain and torture on someone they don't know."

"Torture? Are you telling me he might've still been alive when his eyes were gouged out?"

"It's hard to tell. Maybe the assailant did it directly after he was killed. Pure speculation either way, until I get a chance to examine him properly."

"I don't suppose you've discovered any ID on him, have you?" Katy glanced around. All she could see were four SOCO team members and the two uniformed officers at either end of the crime scene, ensuring no other cars came closer than was necessary. "No witnesses either by the look of things."

"That's where you're wrong, on both counts. There's a man in the back of one of the squad cars, he called it in to your lot. I asked him to stick around when I got here, knowing that you'd want to speak to him. And the victim's ID is in an evidence pouch, sitting by my bag."

"Okay, Charlie, why don't you go and question the man? See if he saw anyone hanging around, either on foot or if he noticed another car in the vicinity."

Charlie nodded and set off.

Katy took a few steps over to the right and snapped on a pair of latex gloves, then bent down to pick up a clear evidence bag. "A wallet, well, what do you know?" She opened it and searched inside. His driving licence gave her all the information she needed. Katy jotted down the man's name and address in her notebook, which she struggled to remove from inside her suit, then she replaced the wallet in the bag and returned to where Patti was crouching next to the corpse.

"Any good?" Patti asked.

"Yep, I've got his name and address, I'll run it through the satnav. I don't think he was too far from home, judging by the postcode I used to get out here."

"That's a shame. Maybe the perp was waiting for him, anticipating his arrival and pounced."

"Seems a pretty logical theory to me. What else can you tell me? All that blood on his shirt, that wouldn't just be from his eyes, would it?"

"No. He has several puncture wounds all over his chest."

"Puncture wounds? Any idea what the perp's choice of weapon could have been?"

"Something long and thin would be my guess at this time."

"Long and thin, eh? Such as?"

"A large needle, knitting needle possibly, or even, dare I say it, an ice pick."

"Jesus, do people genuinely carry around either of those things on a daily basis?"

"Not to my knowledge, which would back up my account of the perp lying in wait, ready to pounce."

"So, premeditated?"

"Definitely, at least that's what the evidence is leading me to believe at present."

"How many times was he stabbed, roughly?"

"I haven't had a chance to move him yet. Let me get the photos snapped off first and then I can turn him over, see what we can find there. Jeff, any chance you can get your finger out and get the pics taken, man?"

Jeff raised a hand and shouted, "Sorry, Patti. The camera is playing up. I'm trying to fix it. I shouldn't be long."

Patti cringed. "That's all we ruddy need. Jeff, leave it and grab the one off the passenger seat in my van. I can't wait around all day. Some of us want to get home to their beds tonight."

"I hear you. Doing it now, Patti."

Katy sniggered, and Patti narrowed her eyes at her.

"Don't you start. Seriously, if men had brains, the world would be a bloody dangerous place to live in, I swear it would."

"Don't be too harsh on him, Patti, he was doing his best to fix it."

"Bollocks, I'm always telling him off about fiddling with the equipment." She lowered her voice. "He's one of these types who insist on knowing how things work and takes great pleasure in taking things apart and putting them back together again. I'm not surprised the damn thing has given up the ghost and stopped working. Grr…he's got me all worked up now. Today has been long enough as it is and…" She waved a hand to dismiss her anger. "Sorry, you don't want to hear me whinge on about work colleagues."

"Fill your boots. It's better to vent about these things than let them surface as an ulcer, love."

"Thanks, you're too kind."

Patti and Katy stepped back a few paces when Jeff finally materialised. He fired off dozens of photos of the victim, taken from different angles, some low to the ground and some with him towering above. Once he'd finished, he gave Patti the thumbs-up.

"Great, thanks." Patti returned to the corpse and removed the eyes, slotting them into another evidence bag which she handed to Katy.

"Gee, I really appreciate your thoughtfulness."

Patti grinned. "Thought you might. Let's turn him over and see what we've got."

"Do you need a hand?"

"Nope, I've got this. Right." Patti hoisted the man over onto his stomach and assessed the wounds on his back. "Only two puncture wounds, here and here. Seems to me, he was probably running from his attacker and then, what, ran out of puff? His courage emerged, and he decided to face the onslaught head-on? Hard to tell, could be either of those scenarios. Either way, it resulted in his death. An incredibly gruesome one at that."

"Any signs of him fighting back?"

Patti checked under the man's fingernails and shook her head, then placed a bag over each of the victim's hands. "Nothing, but just in case there's something lingering under there."

"Poor man. So he was attacked in the middle of nowhere, not far from home. How often does that happen out here in the sticks?"

"My guess would be not that often at all. Still none the wiser as to who might have killed him. I can't see any evidence or DNA around."

"Why am I not surprised about that? Criminals are getting smarter by the day, too many CSI programmes on the TV. Probably guilty of giving the perps ideas how to kill their victims, I shouldn't wonder."

"All right, steady on. Let's not cast aspersions just yet, not before I've carried out the PM."

Charlie joined them, her notebook in her hand.

"Anything, Charlie?" Katy asked, her expectations rising.

"The gent was out for an evening walk and stumbled across the scene. He rang nine-nine-nine right away. Poor bloke said he puked over in the hedge not far from the victim. Had trouble holding it in, apparently."

"Never mind, as long as we're aware, eh, Patti?"

"Yep, always good to know."

"I take it he didn't see any vehicles in the vicinity at all?" Katy asked.

Charlie sighed. "Nope, nothing at all. He's really sad. Dale Peters is one of his neighbours."

"Shit! That's tough. Could he tell you anything about the victim?"

Charlie flipped over a page. "He lives at four Downey Crescent, only a few miles up the road. He's married to Adele and has five kids."

"Fuckity fuck," Patti said, letting out a whistle. "The poor wife is going to be devastated when she hears."

"No kidding," Katy added. "Five kids! Shit, I'm not looking forward to breaking the news. Bummer. The witness didn't call the wife, did he?"

"No, he was tempted but thought better of it. Didn't want that particular conversation preying on his mind for the rest of his life is how he put it."

"I don't blame him either. Crap. Okay, anything else, Charlie?"

"Nope, that's about it from me."

"All right, well, if you've got nothing else for us, Patti, we'd better go and break the news to his wife. Bloody hell, why did I have to take this case?"

Patti rubbed Katy's arm to comfort her. "Now then, I have faith in you, Katy. You've got this."

"Yeah, okay, I think I'll be all right. Piss, after a long day at work, I just hope I don't make any mistakes and mess everything up. It's hard enough telling a loved one their spouse isn't coming home again, let alone adding that he died a gruesome death."

"My advice would be not to tell her. She won't know about his eyes until any court case, there's no need for her to hear about that from you, or me for that matter. Let's not cloud the image she has of her husband."

"Thanks. Come on, Charlie, let's make a move before darkness descends."

"I was thinking the same, we need to get a wriggle on and get this young, I'm using the term loosely here, man's body back to base."

"Will you do the PM tonight or leave it until the morning?" Katy asked.

"I'll leave it. I'm shagged." Patti grinned widely.

Katy and Charlie walked back to their cars and stripped off their protective suits. After depositing them into the black sack at the perimeter of the crime scene, they got back in their respective cars and began their onerous journey, having to turn back the way they had come to take another route to get to the Peters' house.

Katy was impressed by the pretty pink cottage, the way it seemed to proudly dominate the plot it sat within. The quaint windows were topped off by a newly thatched roof which appeared to be the hair of the home but lacking a parting. Getting out of their vehicles, Katy sighed and said, "Lovely. This would be Mum and Dad's ideal retirement home, not that they could afford anything as grand as this. It's huge."

"Well, their neighbour did say they have five kids. I suppose it has to be on the large side to fit seven people."

"True enough. Can't wait to see inside. Shit, what am I saying? I should bloody be preparing myself for the worst undertaking possible, and here I am, admiring the gaff and wondering what the inside looks like. Shame on me."

"Don't be so hard on yourself, it's human nature."

"Let's get on with it. Notebook to hand; let's hope she can at least give us a clue or two as to who would carry out such a vile act on her husband."

"We can live in hope, right?" Charlie's expression was one of doubt, not hope.

"PMA when we go in there, if at all possible."

Entering the garden via the squat wrought-iron gate, they strode up the narrow path with its display of cottage plants in a spectrum of colours, surrounding the patches of lawn on either side. Katy rang the bell, and they waited for the door to be answered. A blonde girl with pigtails, dressed in dungarees and a checked shirt, answered it a few seconds later.

"Hi, is your mum at home?"

Her eyes narrowed, and suspicion was evident in her tone. "Yeah, she might be. Who are you?"

Katy held up her ID. "We're from the Met Police, DI Foster and DC Simpkins. Would you mind getting her for me, please?"

"Just a minute. I'm going to have to shut the door, Mum won't allow me to let strangers into the house."

"Do what you have to do."

The door slammed, and the teenager's shouting filtered out in the distance. The door was reopened a few moments later by a woman in her fifties. She seemed harassed and swept back a clump of hair that had escaped the bun sitting atop her head. She wiped her hands on the tea towel she was holding and frowned.

"Sorry, who are you? My daughter said you're the police, is that right?"

"It is, Mrs Peters. Would it be possible for us to come in for a moment to speak with you?"

"Now isn't a good time. We're all running late. None of us have had dinner yet. My husband is delayed, Lord knows why, he hasn't had the decency to ring me, but then, that's nothing new. I've not long been in from work myself, and the kids...sorry, you don't want to hear this crap. What's this about?"

"Inside would be better."

She stood behind the oak door and allowed them to enter. "You'll have to speak to me while I finish preparing the cottage pie in the kitchen."

"No problem."

She led the way through the dimly lit hallway out to a large, bright extension at the back.

"This is lovely." Katy admired the structure which was predominantly made from glass and overlooked a spacious patio filled with an abundance of colourful pots.

"Thank you. It's a new addition from three years ago. We spend most of our time out here instead of the lounge, which is very dark by comparison. Can I get you a drink?"

Katy smiled. "Thanks, but we'll decline your kind offer, if you don't mind." She glanced over her shoulder to see five children of varying ages, anything from the teenage girl who had answered the door to a small boy of around three or four who was playing with a set of cars on the leather sofa in the TV area of the spectacular room.

"That's up to you. Do you want to take a seat while I prepare the veggies?" Mrs Peters picked up a bag of carrots and carried them over to the marble-topped island a few feet away. She motioned at the stools tucked under the lip on the other side.

"Thank you. It would be better if you gave us your full attention." Katy swallowed back the acid burning her throat. She knew that this woman's world was about to be changed in an instant, and here she was, none the wiser, trying to do her best to look after her family's needs.

Adele put the knife down and pushed the carrots to the side. "Okay, you've got it."

Katy peered over her shoulder at the children and lowered her voice. "Perhaps it would be better if the children left the room, Mrs Peters."

"What? No, you can't ask me to tell them to leave. Just get on with it. You've disrupted our evening enough as it is. Say what you have to say and be on your way."

Katy stared at her in disbelief, fearing she'd handled this all wrong. She clasped her hands together and placed them on the worktop. "Okay, it is with regret that we have to share the news that your husband's body was found half…" She didn't get any further because Mrs Peters fainted.

Katy and Charlie leapt off their stools to tend to the woman. The kids all started either shouting or screaming. The older girl, who had opened the door to them, rushed to her mother's aid and fell to her knees.

"Mummy, please, Mummy, wake up." She looked up, glared at Katy and shouted, "Why are you telling such lies? Our dad, where is he?"

Katy kneeled beside her and reached out two fingers to feel her mother's neck for a pulse. It was thumping well, which came as a relief. "What's your name?"

"Trina. Please, you have to help her. Is it true?" Her eyes widened and glistened with unshed tears.

"One thing at a time. Why don't you help me to make your mother more comfortable?"

"How? Oh God, I can't deal with this shi… Jacob, get the others upstairs. We'll see to Mum, don't worry, she's going to be fine."

Katy smiled at the teenager and nodded. "Yes, she will."

One of the older boys rounded up his siblings and marched them out of the room and up the stairs.

"Charlie, help me lift her onto the sofa."

Together, they hoisted the woman off the floor and crossed the room, depositing her on the sofa where Trina positioned a furry cushion under her head.

Trina then ran back to the kitchen area and filled a glass with water. She returned and placed it on the coffee table and stared down at her mother. The tears fell. Charlie tried to comfort the poor girl with an arm around her shoulder, but she was having none of it and shrugged her off.

"Why isn't she coming around yet? How long does it take?"

"As long as the body needs to take to recover from the shock. I'm sorry you had to witness this," Katy replied, a burning sensation heating her chest.

"What if she dies as well?"

The words gave Katy a sucker punch to her solar plexus. She shook her head. "We mustn't think like that. Let's try and bring her around. I don't suppose you have any smelling salts here?"

"What's that?" Trina asked, her innocence coming to the fore.

"Never mind."

"Will vinegar do the trick?" Charlie asked.

"It might do. Look in the cupboards, Charlie." Katy pointed back into the kitchen.

"No, there, on the dining table. Dad has it on his meals every night," Trina told them.

Katy smiled at Trina, and Charlie went to collect the bottle. She handed it to Katy who removed the top and wafted it under Mrs Peters' nose.

"What's your mother's name, Trina?"

"Adele."

Katy kicked herself, she knew that, Charlie had told her that much back at the crime scene after she'd spoken to the neighbour. She'd merely forgotten when all the drama had kicked off. "Adele, can you hear me?"

Nothing. The woman's eyes didn't flutter at all. No movement in any of her limbs either.

Katy tilted the bottle onto her fingers and dabbed the vinegar under Adele's nose. Then she shook the woman's shoulder gently and called her name over and over.

Finally, after a few minutes of trying, Adele's eyes opened a touch. Trina flew into her mother's arms and broke down.

"Mum, Mum, we thought we'd lost you."

"Hush now, child. Give me some room to breathe. I'm all right."

Trina kissed her mother on the cheek and took a few steps back.

"How are you?" Katy handed Adele the glass of water.

Adele slowly sat up and took a sip from the glass. "Tell me what happened to him, to my Dale."

Katy turned to look at Trina. "Maybe you should go check on your brothers and sisters."

"Mum? Should I leave you?"

"Yes, love. I'll be all right in a second or two." Adele swung her legs off the sofa and onto the floor and took a larger sip of water.

The three of them watched Trina stomp out of the kitchen and listened to her thunder up the stairs to the room above to be with the rest of the children.

Katy smiled at the woman. "I'm so sorry to cause you so much stress. It's never easy giving someone this kind of news."

"I've never fainted before. The shock was too much." She held up her wrist and studied her gold watch. "He should have been home long ago. I didn't realise it was so late. I've only been home an hour myself. By the time I sorted the kids out with their homework—a couple of them had a few problems with their maths—it was time to start on dinner. I haven't even bothered looking at the clock since I got home."

"You lead a busy life, it's understandable. What job do you do?"

"I'm a secretary at the university where my husband works. Saying that, our paths rarely cross during the day. He's busy giving lectures, and I'm situated in an office at the other end of the complex. That's by the by. What happened? Was it an accident?"

Katy shook her head. "I'm sorry to have to tell you that we believe your husband was murdered."

Adele held her gaze, and her mouth dropped open. She shook her head as if to recover from the shock. "My God, no, not Dale. Do you know who? Where did this happen, at the university? Was it one of the students? No, it couldn't be, could it?"

"We don't know. We've come directly from the scene. Our first task is always to inform the next of kin. Are you up to answering a few questions?"

"Of course. I mean, I think so, there's no telling if I'm going to pass out again or not. Bloody hell, this has come as such a shock. Murdered? I find it incredible to believe. Do you think it's one of those road rage incidents? My husband has always been a careful driver, never one to cause problems behind the wheel, not to my knowledge anyway."

"We're unclear about the circumstances, as you can imagine, being out here there weren't any witnesses. I have to tell you, bearing that in mind, it could prove very difficult to solve your husband's case."

"What? You can't tell me that. What nonsense. How dare you say such a thing? Are you telling me that you're going to give up at the first hurdle? Not bother investigating his death?"

"No. I didn't say that. Sorry, of course we're going to give it our very best shot, that goes without saying. What I meant was, without witnesses or evidence, our undertaking is going to be that much harder."

"I see. In that case, I'm sorry for snapping. What a bloody mess. How the hell am I going to bring up five kids on my own, what with me working full-time?" She waved a hand, dismissing her own statement. "Ignore me, I'm being selfish, thinking of myself when I should be thinking of my dear husband. Please forgive me."

Katy shook her head. "Seriously, there's nothing to forgive. I can't predict what your life is going to be like in the future but I'm sure the kids will pull you through this and help out as much as they can. Do you have any relatives in the area?"

"Unfortunately, both sets of parents are now dead. All I have is an elderly aunt who lives in a care home. She won't be able to help, she barely remembers my name most of the time."

"Sorry to hear that. What about friends or your neighbours?"

"Yes, they'll probably do their best to help out now and again. It doesn't matter, that's not your concern. I need to know how he died?"

"You don't. It wasn't very pleasant. I'd rather save you from knowing that, if it's all the same."

Adele stared at her hands in her lap and whispered, "Did he suffer?"

"We have no way of telling, not until the post-mortem results are in," Katy lied. It was only a white lie, saving the woman from yet more anguish.

"Why? Was he robbed?"

"No. His wallet was found on him at the scene. There was money inside, so we're going to rule out that scenario. Has your husband had any problems at work or in his personal life in the last few weeks?"

Adele contemplated the question for a while and then glanced up at Katy, her head swishing from side to side. "No. If he did have any then he kept them from me." She ran a hand around her face. "I can't believe he's gone. He was such a wonderful father. Not bad considering when we first met, he told me he didn't want kids. Then, once he held Trina in his arms for the first time, he was smitten. Couldn't wait to have more. If I hadn't told him that five was enough, he would have wanted a whole tribe of them, not that five isn't a tribe."

"He was a devoted father then?"

"Yes, and some. All his spare time was spent with the kids. He never ventured out on his own to the pub with friends or anything like that. He adored the children and was always voicing his disgust at the men who walked out on their families without a second thought of the struggle their wives or partners would go through bringing the kids up alone. And now, I'm left to do just that. If I know my husband, he would have fought tooth and nail for that not to happen. Is that how he died? Defending our reputation?"

"We're unsure of the facts. I'll tell you what we do know. He lost his life a few miles from the house."

She gasped. "No. He was nearly home? Is that what you're telling me?"

"I'm afraid so. Someone attacked him. He had several wounds, which tells us it was a prolonged attack. The pathologist who attended the scene believes that your husband possibly knew his killer. Which is why I asked if your husband has had any problems or fallings out with anyone recently."

Fresh tears gathered and dripped onto her cheeks. "No, I don't think so. Why would he fall out with someone? He had his family. He no longer had what you'd call close friends. He did back in the day, but nowadays, like I said, it was his choice to be at home with me and the kids. We used to go away one weekend a month, take the tent and go off camping. The kids loved to do that. To spend valuable time with him, and he loved to be around us all."

"You say he was a lecturer. May I ask what subject he taught?"

"He was an English literature professor. He cherished the job he had and was blessed to have good students. Some of them have gone on to become famous authors. He was thrilled to have had a hand in their success. A couple of them even went out of their way to visit him, to hand him a signed copy of their books." She darted off the sofa and went over to the pine bookcase in the corner. She returned clutching five paperbacks. She flipped a few of them open and showed them to Katy and Charlie. "You see, each one has written a special note, thanking him for his wonderful teaching over the years. He was so proud to see the success they had achieved thanks to his lectures."

"Those must have been wonderful and satisfying endorsements for him to receive."

"Yes. So why would anyone want to rid a man like that of his precious livelihood, let alone his life? None of this makes sense." She covered her face, and her shoulders moved up and down rhythmically as her sobbing filled the room.

Katy cringed and glanced over at Charlie who was shifting uncomfortably on the spot.

"I'm sorry to put you through this at such a sad time. I really appreciate what you're telling us. Can I get you anything?"

"A tissue," she mumbled, wiping her nose on the sleeve of her colourful jumper.

Charlie raised a finger, indicating she would see to it, and returned with a couple of sheets of kitchen roll.

"Thank you," Adele said, after blowing her nose. "Oh God, what a sad week this has turned out to be."

"In what way?" Katy asked.

"Only a few days ago, my husband was a pallbearer at one of his oldest friend's funerals, and now this…"

Katy stared at Charlie and then back at Adele. "What was the name of his friend?"

"Bruce, um, let me think. Yes, Bruce Crawford. I had a prior engagement so I couldn't attend the funeral."

Katy's heart tempo increased significantly, forcing her to take a seat.

"Oh my, we're aware of Bruce's death. We're also in the process of investigating his murder."

"No!"

6

"What the…? Did you know Bruce?" Katy's mouth dried up. She didn't know how she got the words out with the lack of saliva present.

"Not really. Dale was friends with him before I came along. That's why I didn't feel up to attending the funeral. Murdered, you say? How is that possible? Both of them gone within a few days?"

"I don't know but I intend to find out. We're going to have to make a move now, if you're sure you're going to be okay?"

She sniffled and wiped her nose on a second piece of kitchen towel. "Yes, I have Trina and the other children to help me pull through this. Will you keep me informed?"

"Of course. I really do hate leaving you like this, but we have a killer to catch."

"Go, please, don't worry about me." She rose from the sofa and showed them to the front door. "Who do you think is doing this and why?" Her eyes shone through the tears.

"At this stage I have no idea. We'll go back to the station now and put our heads together with our team, see what we can come up with. Hopefully, we'll catch the person soon, we have to."

"I have faith in you, you seem a very capable officer."

"I like to think so. Take care, and again, you have my sincere condolences."

"Thank you." She closed the door gently behind them.

Katy dug Charlie with her elbow. "Come on, we need to get on the phone and call the team back. Are you all right to pull some overtime tonight?"

"Sure. I'll ring Brandon after I've contacted the rest of the team."

"Good. You do that from the car while I ring Roberts, he'll need to sanction the overtime. I can't see him objecting to it in the circumstances. Then I'll have to call home and break the news to AJ. Bugger, our lives are all work at the moment and no play. Not sure I'm liking this much. Will we ever get used to it?"

"I doubt it. I look at it this way, as long as I'm busy and the time passes quickly, then I'm fine with it."

"That's logical, Charlie, well said."

"Shall I leave my car here? I can pick it up later."

Katy thought it was a strange statement but accepted Charlie's decision, thinking she might have wanted to unburden some puzzling thoughts on the way back to the station. "If that's what you want?"

Charlie got in Katy's car, and Katy remained outside to speak to Roberts. "Hi, it's Katy, sir, sorry to disturb you."

"You're disturbing my microwave meal for one. This had better be good, Inspector."

"Oops, anything nice?"

"Inspector…say what you have to say and leave me to get on with it."

His tone held a warning that he wasn't in the mood for a discussion on his choice of meals. Neither was she, truth be told.

"A quick summary for you then: I need you to authorise overtime for this evening, sir. Charlie and I have just left the home of a second victim in our murder enquiry."

"What? Are you telling me you're dealing with two murders now?"

"That's what I said, yes, sir."

"Jesus, and you think they're connected, how?"

"After speaking to the second victim's wife, she dropped the bombshell that both men knew each other and her husband was actually a pallbearer at Bruce Crawford's funeral the other day."

"Whoa! Seriously? What's running through your mind, Katy?" he asked, finally climbing down off his high horse.

"I'm not sure. I have an inkling but I need proof or at least some evidence to back my suspicions up. At present, all that is lacking."

"Go on, what are you thinking?"

"Forgive me. I'd rather not say at this point. I'm not that keen of having egg plastered over my face."

"What if I ordered you to tell me, would you?"

Katy blew out a breath. "You could try."

"DI Foster, I'm ordering you to share your suspicions on this extremely perplexing investigation."

"In that case, sir, you leave me no option than to say, I think the daughter has something to do with this."

"How sure are you?"

"At least ninety percent at this stage."

"That's not good enough, not to act upon. If you need to bring her in for questioning, I would caution you to do so with care."

"I'm aware of the pros and cons of working on instinct. I was privy to it whilst serving with my previous partner, if you remember. Maybe some of her shenanigans have finally rubbed off on me."

He sniggered. "Let's hope you don't pick up on too many of her traits, like how she used to speak and deal with me."

"No, sir. I'll be sure not to go down that route. I respect you for one thing."

"Ha! Are you saying Lorne didn't?"

"I think I've said too much already. Getting back to the reason I've rung you, is it okay to forge ahead with the overtime?"

"Yes, of course. Keep me updated every step of the way. Umm… maybe not *every* step, every significant step, I should have said."

"You know that goes without saying, sir. Enjoy the rest of your evening."

"I will. Damn, I'll have to reheat my dinner now…or maybe I'll just put it in the bin where I should have dumped it in the first place."

"May I ask what it was?"

"Chicken tikka served with bullet rice, at least that's what it damn well tastes like. I'm going to have to get a woman in."

"To cook your meals?"

"Yes, why, what else did you think I was talking about, Inspector?"

"Umm…is that the time? I should get going, sir. I hope you sort your dinner out soon."

"I will. Tread carefully. Make sure you gather all the evidence first and foremost before tackling the daughter."

"Thanks for the advice, boss."

"Maybe say that without the added sarcasm attached next time, Inspector."

"I'll try. Goodbye, sir." Katy ended the call and looked over at Charlie to give her the thumbs-up. Then she checked in with AJ to break the bad news to him. "Sorry, love. It's a necessity."

"Stop apologising. I know you wouldn't make the call if you didn't deem it important. Thanks for ringing me."

"Goes without saying. Will you give Georgie a kiss for me?"

"She's here. Hang on. Say hello to Mummy, sweetpea."

"Mummy, I had fun at school today. I made a new friend."

Unexpectedly, Katy's eyes watered. She smiled. "Did you, sweetie? What's her name?"

"It's Jack, and she's a boy."

Katy covered her eyes and chuckled. "Oh, silly Mummy, presuming all your friends should be girls."

"Pre, pre…what's that?"

"Presuming…umm… thinking it should be something when it turns out to be something else. Does that make sense?"

"Er…sort of. I need to go now, my ice cream is melting."

"You go, darling. I'll see you later."

AJ came back on the line. "Hi, you know what she's like with a bowl of ice cream. She was hungry so I fed her earlier."

"I'm so sorry to disrupt your lives the way I do."

"Nonsense, you do nothing of the sort. Hey, you go, stay safe, and remember we love you."

"I love you, too. I'll never know why you put up with me at times."

"Are you nuts? Because we care and love you. I can't wait to see you. I have some news that will cheer you up."

Just like that, he ended the call, leaving her dangling. She was tempted to ring him back and force the information out of him, but they had an important job to do and time was getting on—it was already seven-twenty. She slipped into the driver's seat and started the engine. Charlie finished her call and sighed.

"That was the final one. The team are all on their way back to the station."

"Good, you guys are the best. Was Brandon okay about you working late?"

"Yeah, I think so. He didn't really complain."

Katy picked up an underlying hidden meaning in Charlie's words and tone. She continued to take the detour back to the station and cast a glance sideways to see Charlie staring down at her fingers, picking at the skin around her nails. "Is there something you're not telling me, Charlie?"

"No, I'm fine. We have some issues to work out. It's part and parcel of being involved in a relationship. Nothing spectacular, just tiny issues."

"Yeah, we all have those. It's not helped by the guilt we feel either, is it?"

"Maybe that has more to do with how I'm feeling. Just ignore me, I'm sure Brandon and I will be fine."

Katy held her fingers up. "I'm here to use as a sounding board if you should ever need one."

"I know. Ditto."

"AJ has some news for me. He's such a tease, told me that then hung up."

"You guys have the best relationship. I wish mine and Brandon's was half as good as yours."

"Are you telling me you're not as solid as you used to be?"

"Is anyone? I thought it was the norm for relationships to settle into...well, something more comfortable."

"Don't let your mother hear you talking like that. Charlie, after what you've been through, you deserve to be treated like a princess every second of the day."

"Aww...now you're making me out to be some kind of ogre. Brandon treats me better than any other guy I've been out with, not that there have been that many. Ignore me, I'm sure we'll be fine. If not..." Charlie shrugged. "Then I'll have good memories to look back on."

Katy's eyes widened. "Bloody hell. That sounds like you've given up on either the relationship or Brandon."

"Did it? Sorry, I haven't. Can we talk about something else? This conversation is making me squirm."

"Whatever you want. What are your feelings on the investigation so far?"

"Thanks, I'm not sure which conversation is the more demanding."

They both laughed.

"If there is a connection, which it sure looks like to me, then maybe the men had a secret. Something their families weren't aware of," Charlie noted.

"Am I to believe you don't think Nadia is to blame here?"

"Why should we? What's she actually said or done to make you think she might be guilty of something?"

"Good point. I can't rid myself of this damn feeling in my gut."

"What do you propose doing about it?"

"I'd rather not dive in and regret my actions. I want to run things past the team first."

"Makes sense to me. We'll back your decision either way, you know that."

"I know. On the flip side, I would hope you'd tell me if you thought I was playing the wrong cards during an investigation as well."

"I would, sort of. Maybe I'd point out a few discrepancies in your way of thinking, now that I've worked with you a couple of months and know how approachable you are."

"My job is done then. I'm glad you feel that way, Charlie." She leaned to her side and whispered, "I think we make a pretty shit-hot partnership."

Charlie laughed. "You took the words out of my mouth."

*T*he team showed up within half an hour of each other. Charlie ensured everyone had a cup of coffee to hand while Katy filled in the necessary details on the whiteboard.

She turned to face her team. "Thank you all for returning to work this evening. I hope the quick turnaround hasn't affected your home lives too much. Please send my apologies to your loved ones. Right, as you're aware by now, Charlie and I were called out to attend yet another murder scene this evening. It was a gruesome one. The victim had several stab wounds across his chest and to his back as well. My suspicion is that he was possibly in the process of running away from his assailant. There were two separate areas of blood spatter to back this idea up, too. His eyes were also gouged out and left to rest on his chest."

"Yuck, not pleasant," Karen muttered.

"No, not in the slightest. The intriguing part is that when we went to break the news to his wife, she informed us that her husband, Dale Peters, knew this man." She pointed at the first victim's name on the board with the marker pen. "Bruce Crawford. So that's where we need to start digging. How did these men know each other, and what did they do to make someone so angry with them that they chose to exact their revenge?"

"Any clues at all as to where we should be digging, boss?" Patrick asked.

"At this stage, no. Anything and everything you can find. Links to their jobs, the types of interests they held, I want it all. I'm going to ring Nadia, request a meeting with her, see what she can tell us. Let's hit the computers hard and fast on this one, folks."

Katy left the team and walked into her office. She searched for Nadia's number and rang it. It immediately went to voicemail.

Is she at work? Or at home? I need to speak with her, urgently!

She took a punt and rang the hospital. The ward sister informed her that Nadia had finished her shift several hours earlier at six o'clock. Katy's head spun.

Six o'clock, so it would have been possible for her to have driven out to the murder scene and to have committed the crime, wouldn't it?

She searched for a home number for the woman—she didn't have one, and there was no telling if she even had one either. Most people tended to have a mobile number these days without the necessity of having a landline. She pushed her chair back and sped out of the office. "Charlie, let's go."

Charlie unhooked her jacket from her chair and followed Katy out of the incident room. They flew down the stairs, brushed past several of their colleagues and out to the car.

"I take it we're going to see Nadia?" Charlie hopped into the passenger seat as soon as the doors unlocked.

"That's right. Something is way off to me. I know I keep saying it but…I rang her mobile, no answer. So I tried the hospital. They told me she left work at around six."

"Holy moley! You're thinking she would've had enough time to have driven out to the crime scene and killed Peters."

"It makes sense to me."

"Want me to ask a member of the team to check the ANPRs, see if they can spot her car?"

"Good thinking. Ask Graham to do it, would you? He's got more experience than the others with that side of things."

Charlie made the call and put Graham to work. He said he'd contact them as soon as he found anything.

Katy drew up outside Nadia's house.

Charlie pointed at her car. "She's home."

"Well, her car is here, that's a good sign. Come on. Let's see what she has to say for herself."

Katy approached the front door with her heart hammering against her ribs.

"Are you all right?" Charlie whispered.

"Yeah, maybe feeling a little hyper. I want this killer caught."

"Understandable. Take a few deep breaths. If that doesn't sound too condescending."

"It doesn't. Good advice." Katy sucked in several breaths and let them out slowly, then knocked on the door.

Nadia, dressed in a leopard-skin onesie, opened it a few seconds later, an expression of surprise covering her pretty face. "Hello, Inspector. What brings you here at this time of night?"

Katy offered up a tight smile and held the woman's gaze. "Would it be possible for us to come in and speak with you?"

"Of course. Would you like a drink? I was just about to make a coffee when the bell rang."

"No, we'll pass this time around, but thank you anyway."

Once they were in the lounge, Nadia gestured for them to take a seat and left the room. She returned a few moments later carrying a mug and placed it on the coffee table in front of the sofa which was now covered in a fur throw. "You didn't answer me. Am I to take it that you have news about my father's murder?"

"Yes and no. Can I ask what you've been up to today?"

Nadia frowned and took a sip from her drink. "Of course. I worked until six and came straight home. I'm knackered, I've been doing all sorts of weird and wonderful hours lately, mostly to keep my mind off what happened to Dad. I must say, it's helped a lot during the day, however, once I'm at home, I can't stop thinking about him. Finding him in that state and being unable to help him, even with my experience as a nurse." Tears formed, and she quickly brushed them away.

"I can understand how distressing that must be for you. Has your sister returned to Scotland now?"

"Oh yes. She went back home immediately after the funeral."

"I see."

"Do you? I detect a strange tone to your voice, Inspector. Would you mind telling me what this visit is about? Either you have some news regarding the case or…"

"Okay, cards on the table, Miss Crawford. We're no further forward with your father's case. Umm…this evening we were called out to another scene." She watched the woman intently, hoping to see some kind of reaction. She was left wanting because there wasn't one.

"Another scene? What are you saying?"

"This evening we encountered another *murder* scene."

Her hand flew up and covered her chest. It rose and fell rapidly while she gathered her composure. "Oh no, that's terrible. What, and you believe this is connected to my father's? Is that why you've come here tonight?" She recovered and reached for her mug of coffee, taking a small sip.

"In a roundabout way, yes."

"How? What am I missing? Or more importantly, what aren't you telling me?"

"The victim was Dale Peters."

"No! My father's friend? But he was only at the funeral last week and now, he's...he's gone as well. What does this mean?"

"It means we're now investigating two gruesome murders, the second one even worse than what happened to your father. Do you have any thoughts on the matter?"

She shook her head slowly; it rapidly gained momentum. "No, should I? Again, I'm not liking the tone of your voice, Inspector. What are you saying? That you think I had something to do with both murders?"

"No, not in the slightest. We simply have a serious dilemma and believe both murders have to be connected. We're here to ask you if you know of any reason why that would be likely."

"I can't think of any reason. I'm as appalled to hear of Dale's death as I was to see my father lying in this very room with his throat cut. Someone did this, and I was hoping you would have had some news about who that person was by now."

"As were we. Your father's case has gone cold very quickly."

"Are you telling me you've given up?"

"No, we'd never just give up. What I'm saying is the leads that we had surrounding your father's investigation have led us nowhere. However, now a second murder has been committed, and the fact that the two victims knew each other has given us another trail to follow."

"I see. And yet you've chosen to turn up on my doorstep and insist on grilling me as though I have something to do with both deaths. Let me say this in simple terms: nothing could be further from the truth, I assure you. The news you've delivered about Dale has come as an enormous shock to me."

"Did you know him?"

"Not really. Not that I can remember. He and my father used to be friends when I was younger. I'm not sure what happened to end that friendship, but they seemed to drift apart for some reason."

"Please, if you can cast your mind back to around that time, at least it'll point us in the right direction. At the moment, we're struggling to make sense of why two people who knew each other have been murdered."

"Can you tell me how Dale was murdered? You said it was gruesome."

"That's right. No, I'm afraid we can't disclose that. I'm sure once the press get hold of the details it'll be all over the media within the next few days."

"If that's so, then what's the harm in you telling me now? I have a stake in this case, don't I? As in, he died in connection to my father's death. Oh God, hark at me. I'm sorry, this is all coming out wrong. I don't want to hear the ins and outs of Dale's death, why would I? My God, I don't even know why I damn well asked."

"I did wonder. As I said, we can't divulge such information. All you can do to help with the investigation is to think back to when your father and Dale were friends and try and tell us if anything happened back then that could reflect on why someone might want to kill them both."

"I'll have to think about it. You see, in all honesty, because I lost my mother at such a young age, I've tended to block out my childhood. Can you understand that?"

"I think I can. You were four at the time she died, yes?"

"That's right. I suppose I thought blocking her out would be less painful. I don't know if that was the right way of going about things or not. I missed out on having a mother at a very young age. To some kids that might be classed as traumatic."

"Did you have access to a counsellor back then, can you remember?"

"I don't believe so. My father knew what was best for me." Her gaze dropped to the mug she was holding, and she stared at it for a long time then added, "He took over the role of being both mother and father. I suppose most parents would do the same if they found themselves in the same boat."

"I suppose. Speaking with Penny, she seemed to raise some doubts about the way your father raised you both."

"Did she? Penny has always had certain views about our father, views that I wouldn't have necessarily agreed with over the years. She left home as a teenager."

"And yet, you chose to remain living with your father. May I ask why?"

She shrugged. "Apart from the financial side of things, I can't tell you if there was a specific reason behind my wanting to stay with him. Maybe I felt he needed me. Perhaps we needed each other. I don't really know."

"Are you telling me you had a different kind of relationship with your father than your sister had with him?"

She continued to stare at her mug, but her foot tipped over to the side and righted itself numerous times before she responded, "Perhaps. It's hard to tell."

"Is there something you're not telling us, Nadia?" Katy tried to coax her.

The young woman gulped and shook her head several times. "No, definitely not. I'd like to get back to normality as soon as possible. I'm struggling to do that with my father's case still wide open. I need your word that you'll find whoever has done this to my father and Dale. Wasn't he married?"

"Yes, to Adele. We've spoken to her before coming here. As you can imagine, she's distraught by the untimely loss of her husband. She has five children to bring up on her own now."

Nadia gasped. "Oh shit! I didn't know."

Sensing her words meant more than she was letting on, Katy asked, "Would it have made a difference if you'd known?" Katy felt Charlie's gaze burning into her; Katy didn't respond.

Nadia glanced up, her gaze latching on to Katy's. "Meaning?"

"I just wondered. Whether a man is married with a family or not, if that made a difference to the level of sympathy you had for him and his family."

"What a strange statement. That's not how I interpreted what you said at all."

Katy inclined her head and asked innocently, "Oh, I'm sorry, how did you take it?"

Nadia waved a hand in front of her. "It doesn't matter. Will that be all now? It's getting late, and I have an early shift starting at six in the morning."

Katy and Charlie rose from their seats.

"That's fine. I think we're done here. You've got my card. If anything should come to mind regarding your childhood, you will ring me, won't you?"

"I'll be sure to do that. I'll show you out and then go to bed. It's been a very long day, or should I say a long week."

"It's good to keep busy, it must help to take your mind off your father's death."

"Sort of. Goodbye." Nadia closed the front door behind them.

They made their way back to the car in silence.

It wasn't until they'd pulled away from the house that Charlie tutted. "You were a bit close to the line back there, weren't you?"

"Maybe I was, it was intentional. You know what? The more I spend time with that woman, the more I think she has something to hide."

Charlie tutted again. "I'm sorry to go against you but I'm not feeling it. Perhaps that's my inexperience coming through. I'll reserve judgement for now. What's next?"

"Maybe. Trust me, there's something going on with her. We'll go back to the station, see what the others have come up with, if anything, and then call it a day."

"Really? You're throwing in the towel early, aren't you?"

Katy heaved out a sigh. "Not necessarily. If the guys back at base have news for us then it could likely be a long night. If they have nothing, then it's pointless all of us sitting around, keeping our office chairs warm when we could be at home catching up on our sleep."

"I get that. Ignore me then."

Katy faced Charlie and smiled. "I intend to."

"Charming. Hey, mind if I ask you a personal question while we're alone?"

"Go on. If it's too personal I can always refuse to answer. What's on your mind?"

"Nothing to do with the case. I was wondering how things went with your parents the other week. You've never mentioned it in passing."

"Ugh...AJ and me telling them about being married, you mean?"

"Yes, tell me to keep my nose out if you want."

"No, it's fine. There were a few tears from Mum. Dad was all for us doing it on the cheap, but he's got a tight arse anyway. But yeah, Mum took it badly at first until I reminded her that it was our decision to make and we'd been effectively living as man and wife for over five years. She accepted we'd done the right thing after an hour or so. I think Georgie being there definitely helped to calm the choppy waters. Mum doesn't tend to argue in front of her treasured granddaughter. Why do you ask?"

"It's just you mentioned how distraught AJ's parents were initially but hadn't said anything about how your parents had reacted. I'm glad things worked out for you. It's such a strain on a person's well-being when family members fall out. I should know."

Katy rubbed Charlie's knee in support. "I know, love. You went through the mill with your mum and dad. How is your old man?"

"I haven't spoken to him all week. Last time he rang he was pissed and I hung up on him. He always gets so maudlin when he has alcohol running through his system instead of blood."

"That's such a shame. You guys used to be so close, didn't you?"

"We were, once upon a time. I still love him, nothing would ever change that; however, sometimes I find myself detesting him. That's not natural, is it?"

"Of course it is. Don't be so damn hard on yourself. My advice for you would be to do your best in this life, both professionally and personally, so Tom ends up feeling proud of his little princess."

"Groan, I hate that name. I was never really one for playing with dolls as a child. Being called princess evokes images of a young girl happily playing with her Sindy or Barbie dolls. Cringe, that was never me growing up."

"No, from what I remember your mother telling me, your teens involved causing trouble with the gang you hung around with."

"Fuck, don't remind me. Honestly, we were never that bad. We just used to sit around on the odd street corner drinking alcohol we'd badgered someone to buy for us from the offie."

"You're lucky it didn't go against you during your assessment to join the force."

"I would've been mortified if it had. Don't tell me you breezed through your childhood without getting into trouble?"

Katy twisted her lips. "Sorry, that's exactly what I'm going to say. I was a good girl, I still am, apart from having a child out of wedlock, that is."

They both laughed.

"Do you think you were crying out for attention from your folks by falling pregnant?"

"No, I don't think that was the case at all. They were pretty easy-going with me when I was younger, they still are to be fair. They could have ripped me and AJ to shreds after we shared the news with them about the wedding but they didn't resort to that. I don't mind telling you, had they done something as special as that behind my back, I'm not sure I would've reacted with the same forgiveness. Therefore, I take my hat off to them and I'm thankful they're so chilled about life in general."

"Good to hear. It always makes a difference to have parents who are willing to support you, no matter what you get up to."

"You have that in Lorne. I can't say the same about your father because I've only met him once, maybe twice over the years. Your mum was married to Tony when I became her partner, or maybe it was just after. Yes, I think that was it, but they were together all the same. They have to be the strongest couple I've ever met."

"I hate to say this, but I've often wished that Tony was my real dad. Is that an awful thing to say?"

"Any reason why?"

"He's wonderful. A great support to Mum. I can never remember them ever having a cross word with each other. He worships her, always has done. Hey, a bit like AJ and you. You guys are solid, aren't you?"

"I like to think so. Wait, I don't think I told you, AJ and I have been discussing starting up a new business. Correction, not me per se, he'll be doing it when Georgie is at school full-time."

"That's amazing. What would the business entail?"

"Organising entertainment for children's parties."

"Sounds interesting. Will you run it together?"

"No way, I have enough on my plate as it is. No, it was his idea. Saying that, I'll support him every step of the way. I'll probably get roped in somewhere along the line, no doubt."

"How cool. How did he come up with the idea?"

"Haven't got the foggiest. He just announced it one day and did the research needed. We still have to source a way of funding it. Grr... he hinted earlier that he had some news. I wonder what that's all about. Never mind, I'll find out soon enough, when we eventually get home. Let's hope that's sooner rather than later, because I'm shattered already. What about you?"

"Ditto. Wishing you and AJ well on your forthcoming project. If you don't mind me saying, can't he get his parents to back him?"

"Neither of us want to resort to that. He's not had the best relationship with his parents since he signed up with the Met."

"That's such a shame. Have you run the idea past them? Maybe this would be a good time to mend a few broken bridges. What do you think?"

"Possibly. Let's see what he has to say first, and if that sounds negative, I'll urge him to have a word with his folks."

*T*he incident room was dead quiet when they walked in.

"Everything all right, guys? I expected more activity than this to be honest with you."

Karen glanced up from her computer and smiled. Her eyes were half-closed and red raw. "We've dug and dug, boss, and come up with bugger all. We just don't know where to turn next."

"Okay, I suggest we all call it a day and start over tomorrow. I just told Charlie in the car I'm exhausted. We're not going to do ourselves any favours sticking around here if the information is going to be increasingly hard to find. You all look dead on your feet anyway."

"Cheers for that, boss. Are you sure? We could stumble across a clue at any minute," Graham said.

"Yeah, and we could get hit by an out-of-season snowstorm. I think we should call it a day and gather our thoughts in the morning. I'll leave you with this snippet before we go. We visited Nadia and told her Dale Peters had been murdered. She appeared to be shocked by the news. I'm putting this out there, I still have wavering doubts about her."

"Did she give you an alibi as to her whereabouts this evening?" Patrick asked.

"She did. She left work at around six. I roughly calculated how long it would have taken for her to have driven out to the murder scene. I have to admit the timing was tight, but in my eyes, still doable."

"Are you telling us that we should be concentrating our efforts on her, boss?" Karen asked, tapping her pen against her face.

Katy hitched up a shoulder. "Unless anything else comes our way in the meantime. At present, we've got nothing to back up my claims except a gut feeling that refuses to take a hike. It's annoying the frigging hell out of me, if you must know. I've never had such a strong sense about someone before, and I have no idea why or where it's coming from. I hope to God I'm wrong, but until we find any evidence stating otherwise, then I'm stuck with it."

"Gut instinct isn't essentially a bad thing," Graham replied, his brow wrinkled into a deep frown.

"I know. It's just not the way I work. You know how much it used to get to me when Lorne used to spout about it. Come on, switch the equipment off and go home, again."

She didn't have to repeat herself. The team leapt out of the chairs, switched off their computers and rushed out of the door.

She laughed at Charlie. "Do you think it was something I said?"

"Possibly. All right if I follow them? I'll cadge a lift from Graham to pick up my car."

"Go for it, I'll be right behind you. I just want to make a few notes on the board while they're fresh in my mind."

Charlie wagged a finger. "Don't be too long. Maybe I should stay with you, make sure you go home at a reasonable hour."

"Honestly, there's no need for you to be concerned. You go. I'll see you in the morning."

"Goodnight. Stick to your word, please."

"I will. Drive safely."

7

*S*he hid, shielded by the door to the room in the cellar. She'd crept down during the night. The men intent on shouting in the 'den' as they called it, oblivious to her tiny footsteps. She peered through the gap in the door and placed a hand over her mouth. She'd been down here several times in the past few weeks, fascinated by what took place behind this door. Her eyes moistened, and fear prickled her spine. What she saw would remain with her for a lifetime, she knew that. How couldn't it?

The woman screamed until the girl's father bound her mouth with a gag. The woman stared up at him, as if pleading silently to be set free. One after the other, the men took their turn. She was strapped to a table. Each of them climbed on top and humped her, despite her obvious discomfort and fear. None of them attempted to bring a halt to the proceedings.

Her hand tightened over her thin lips as the woman's muffled pleading went unheard, unregistered by the men.

In between, the female tried to buck, to free herself from the bonds tying her to the table, to no avail. She kicked out with her bare feet as each man approached. She caught one or two of them below the belt which earned her a vicious slap. If she'd just lain there and accepted *her fate, she would have been home and dry by now. None of her assailants had any stamina; a couple of thrusts, and they groaned and fell off her, zipped up their trousers and stood back, ready to cheer on the next one.*

Her father leered at the female, bending over now and again to whisper something derisory in the woman's ear. Which set her off, her objections always muffled by the gag strapped across her mouth.

Night after night, the woman was subjected to this kind of torture, and every night, the little girl descended the stairs when she felt it was safe to do so, as if trying to give the female support just by being close.

And after the rapists had finished, the little girl crept back up to bed and hid under the bedclothes, fearing that if they ever found out she knew what went on in the 'den' she'd be next on the list.

Would the men be as heartless as to do to her the things they did to the woman? She was only four, for Christ's sake.

There was no doubt in her mind that day may come in the future. Something she'd need to be wary of as she grew older. But how, how the hell would she be able to prevent these vile men from dipping their wicks? They seemed determined to inflict injury and humiliation on the woman.

On this occasion, her father led the onslaught to the cheers and backslapping of the other men present. The little girl crossed her legs as if trying to help the woman. It failed. The men continued the barrage on her body. She watched the woman's pained expression, the tears continuously rolling down her flushed cheeks. The girl's heart hurt, pained by what was happening, helplessness shrouding her with its unwelcome cloak.

She was tempted to barge in there, to shout at the men, call them all the horrible names her father had called her from time to time, but how would they react to being interrupted, carrying out their warped, mindless and brutal game?

The little girl lingered, her legs crossed now because she was desperate for the loo. Her hand clamped over her mouth, preventing her own screams to match those of the female. Strike after strike to the woman's face and head. The men were angrier than normal this evening. This was no longer a game. They'd upped their ante, each and every one of them. The woman seemed to sense the difference in tonight's game play.

"Who wants to do it?" her father asked.

She was confused. Do what? Each of the men had already had their way with her, what else could he be talking about?

"I don't mind. I'll have a go?" One of the smaller men stepped forward and placed his hands around the woman's throat.

She screamed and bucked like a mule to get him off her. Her head twisted violently from left to right. He backed away, seemingly embarrassed by his actions, and her father encouraged the next man to approach the table. "Come on, she loves it, being on the brink like that."

Brink of what?

The little girl squeezed her eyes shut. The female's cries for help were deadened by the cloth, and then there was nothing. The girl's eyes flew open. The men shouted at each other. The atmosphere had turned horrid. She had to get out of there. She flew up the stairs to the safety of her room. Checked her little sister was still sound asleep—she was.

She covered herself with the quilt, her tiny body trembling, wishing she could have locked the door behind her, knowing it was forbidden to do so. A noise outside alerted her; she strained an ear. Her mother had always called her a nosey beak. She slipped out of the bed and tiptoed across the floor to the window. The overhanging porch roof blocked out some of her view. Beyond that were five men gathered around a car. Four of them carried a rolled-up rug and bundled it into the back of the vehicle. She opened the curtain a little more to get a better look. One of the men turned her way. She dropped the curtain, and fear catapulted her back to her bed.

Footsteps sounded on the stairs. She tucked the quilt up under her chin and closed her eyes as the bedroom door swung open. She sensed her father towering over her, his breath ragged from his exertions. Then he was gone, and the door closed quietly behind him. She waited for a few moments and then tiptoed back to the window in time to see the men parting and the car with the rug in the back driving off.

That day was the last time she saw her mother.

Nadia woke from the dream in a cold sweat. She hadn't had it for years, why now? Why all of a sudden should it prick her conscience and resurface? Why, after all these years? What was the meaning to this?

8

*R*obin Hewitt left the venue and got in his vehicle. Not far from his home, the car behind flashed him several times. He peered at the driver and noticed a hand pointing to the side of the road. Thinking there must be something wrong with his car, he indicated and pulled over. The car stopped a few feet behind him. He got out of his vehicle and approached the driver to see what the problem was. The driver lowered the window.

He bent down to speak to the stranger. "Is there something wrong?"

The driver pointed at the rear of Robin's car. He took a few steps towards his vehicle and removed his mobile from his pocket. Using the torch, he examined every last inch of the car but found nothing out of place.

The door opened behind him.

"I can't see anything. Can you tell me what it was?" he asked without turning around.

Soft footsteps came from behind, and then something hard cracked him on the back of the head. His hand instinctively reached up to investigate the wound. Sticky fluid covered his palm.

"What the fu—?"

Before he could finish his question, another blow struck him. This time it was harder, sending him to his knees.

"Good, that's just where I want you. Start begging for your life."

Dazed with confusion, his vision blurred, he held out a hand. "Please, don't hurt me. Why are you doing this?"

"Out of necessity. You're a worthless, no-good individual and deserve to die for what you did."

"What? I think you've made a mistake. I haven't done anything wrong. Never."

"How easily dickheads like you forget." The stranger raised the metal bar again, and it came down heavily on the top of his head.

Robin curled up into a ball. Something had cracked with the final blow; he hadn't liked the sound of that. "Please, no more. Tell me what you want. Take my wallet, there's not much in it, but take what I have."

"Ha. I don't want your money. I want to see you suffer. To plead with me to save you, and then I want to see the light in your eyes vanish as you take your final insipid breath."

"Why? Why are you punishing me like this for something I haven't done?"

"Oh, you did it all right. That night, you were just as responsible as the others. That poor woman. She didn't deserve to die, not at the hands of you bastards, just out to get a cheap thrill."

His head turned slowly to look at the dark figure, hiding behind the hoodie. "Who are you?"

"What's the problem, don't you recognise me?" the singsong voice replied, taunting him.

"I can't see you. Reveal yourself to me. Let's discuss this."

"What's to discuss? I'm here to avenge the heinous crime you committed. You and your so-called chums. Not once, not twice, but numerous times until things went too far."

"Who are you? How do you know about this?"

"How do I know? I was there. I witnessed first-hand what you and your disgusting mates did all those years ago."

"Why now? After all this time? I've changed, I have a new life. I haven't thought about what happened that night for years."

"Yeah, I'm well aware of what you've become. I've been keeping an eye on you for months. Gone off the female sex, have you? Suddenly realised that deep down you're gay? Don't worry, I'll make sure Nick knows exactly what type of man you were at your funeral. I'll take pleasure in giving him all the details of what went on that night and the frequent nights before that. In the end, he'll be glad you're dead, feel relieved that he'd only had the misfortune to spend a few miserable nights with you."

"No, you don't know what you're saying, we're devoted to each other. He won't believe you. It's in the past. Why revisit the incident after all these years?" His head throbbed, his speech now affected due to the whacks on the head, his words coming out slurred.

"The time has come for…retribution. You will all be punished for the sins of your past. For the way you treated that woman, many times over. Why? Why disrespect her the way you did?"

"I'm sorry, I never wanted to be involved. It was the others, they forced me to do it."

His attacker lowered and looked him directly in the face. He cowered, and the stranger's hot breath bathed the side of his face.

"Don't lie. I was there, remember. I'm well aware of what happened back then. Not once did you show any form of reluctance to joining in. You were a willing participant, so don't bullshit me."

"I wasn't. I objected numerous times, but the others threatened to do all sorts to me if I didn't join in." Another swipe with the bar, this time to the side of his face, and more bones crunched. He cried out, his jaw slack when he touched it, his voice muffled when he said, "You broke my jaw. Please, no more."

"Or what? How are you going to prevent the inevitable? I know you go to church. You're such a frigging hypocrite, begging for God's forgiveness after what you did. The world will be a better place without you. I'll make sure Nick knows all about your filthy little secret. He'll end up being forever in my debt for disposing of you."

"No. You don't know what you're saying. After what went on that night, I turned to God, and He forgave me. If He'd wanted to have punished me, He would've struck me down by now."

"What, like I have? Maybe *I'm* God. You can't see my face; how do you know I'm not your saviour?"

"My God wouldn't punish me the way you are. He seeks out to punish people for their sins that's true, but He wouldn't do it like this, with such…brutality."

"Brutality? Yes, I like that. It fits most sins you've been guilty of throughout your miserable, deceptive life. To marry a woman, to lie to her for years, knowing that you batted for the other side. You think that was right? To rob her of the chance to lead a happy, fulfilling life with another man, someone who would have bent over backwards to have treated her right? Unlike you, you charlatan. You knew from an early age you liked men and still you put your wife through a life of misery. Why? To make up for what you did? Is that how that warped mind of yours worked in the past?" The stranger prodded his temple.

"Ouch! No. You've got it all wrong. My sexuality has nothing to do with what went on that night, I swear it doesn't. Please don't punish me for the sins, I've done my best to put those behind me and move on."

"Make good on? You killed an innocent woman during your repulsive sex games and you think the world will be a better place if you come out of the closet? No, that's not right. It took you almost twenty years to reveal your true sexuality. In the meantime, you put another woman through fucking hell. You're a selfish fucker with a capital S. What *you* want, you seem to get, stepping over other people in the process. I've met your type before. Others like you have met their comeuppance long before you got yours. I'm bored now. Is there anything you wish to say before the lights go out, so to speak?"

"Yes, I want to talk to Nick, to tell him how much I love him."

"Nope. I didn't say I was allowing you a final call. Don't worry, I'll take pleasure in putting him right on a few things."

He sobbed.

∼

*T*he stranger had heard enough. Blow after blow rained down on their target, the man who had ruined so many lives during his own existence. Until his screams and whining could no longer be heard.

The stranger took the bar back to the car and left the man in the road. A new form of roadkill for the scavenging birds to peck at during the night until someone discovered him.

9

*K*aty groaned and glanced at the clock on her bedside table. The green digital face announced the time as five-forty-five.

"Answer the damn phone," AJ complained. He buried his head under the pillow.

"Hi. DI Foster. This had better be good."

"Sorry to bother you at this early hour, ma'am. I've had notification of another murder on your patch, and the pathologist thought it imperative that I call you right away. She's predicting the death is possibly connected to your ongoing investigation."

"Oh right. Okay, you'd better give me the details. Is the pathologist still at the scene?"

"Yes, ma'am." The woman on control gave her the details of the location and hung up.

Katy turned over to cuddle AJ.

He re-emerged from under the pillow and kissed her. "What a way to get woken up in the damn morning."

"I'm sorry, love. I'll have a quick shower and shoot off."

"Want me to make you a drink and some toast? I don't mind."

"No, you go back to sleep, you need your rest."

His eyebrows shot up. "You're the one who could do with a rest. You were barely in five minutes last night before you dropped off to sleep, and now, you're on the move again long before the birds have even crept out of their nests."

Katy smiled and strained her neck to listen. In the distance, she recognised the familiar morning chorus of the birds in residence near to their home. "Nope, they beat me to it, just. I'll try and call you later this morning, if I get the chance. I'm sorry we didn't get around to discussing the news you wanted to share with me regarding the business."

"It can wait. Go. We'll talk about it tonight, depending what time you get home."

"Sorry, AJ. I'll make it up to you, I promise." She kissed him and leapt out of bed.

"I've heard it all before," he grumbled behind her.

She chose to ignore his hurtful comment—whether it had been intended that way or not, she wasn't sure. After suffering a quick tepid shower, she carried her clothes downstairs and got dressed down there rather than disturb AJ a second time.

*T*wenty-five minutes later, she arrived at the scene, which was cordoned off and being patrolled by two constables in uniforms. She flashed her ID. One of them held the tape up for her to duck under. The area up ahead was being lit by mobile floodlights set up by Scenes of Crime Officers even though the sun was fully awake by now.

"Don't come any closer," Patti shouted, stopping dead.

"Why?"

Patti stared and looked her up and down. "You really have to ask me that, Inspector Foster?"

Katy bashed her hands against her thighs. "Sorry, my mistake, I'll correct it right away."

"Grab a suit from the back of my van."

Her lapse in concentration signified how tired she truly was.

She'd never knowingly strolled up to a crime scene in the past without putting on a protective suit. Well, maybe she had, back in her early days when donning one hadn't yet become a formality to her regime.

Suited and booted, she returned to the crime scene and stood alongside Patti. "Shall we start over, now my wrists are black and blue?"

"Bollocks. You'd soon know if I was angry with you, so don't give me that hogwash."

"Bloody hell! Nothing like telling it how it is, Patti. By your pissed-off attitude, I take it you've been here all night."

"More or less, and before you start kicking off, just remember I waited until daylight broke before I decided to get you out of your comfy bed. I've yet to see mine, it's been over twenty-four hours for me."

Katy placed a hand on Patti's arm. "Sorry about that. Let's call a truce, shall we?"

"Done."

"The woman on control said that you're linking the crime to the others. Can I ask why?"

"Pure speculation at this time. Let's call it a hunch. I didn't want another team turning up to this one in case they muddy the waters. It would be best to have you guys involved in this from the outset. That was my logic anyway. Was I right to call you?"

"Only time will tell. What have we got? Apart from a bloody mess."

"ID says he's Robin Hewitt." Patti extracted an evidence bag from a pile near her feet and held it up for Katy to see.

Her mouth dropped open when she saw the man's photo on his licence. "Shit, damn and blast!"

"Don't tell me you know him?"

Katy's nod sped up. "I do. You'll never guess where from."

"Go on, surprise me."

"The first victim's funeral. I'll stand corrected if I'm wrong but I'd swear this man was one of his pallbearers."

"Fuck, really?"

"I'll need to do some digging to get clarification, but yes. Shit, Patti, tell me you've got a time of death for him?"

"I can give you a rough idea; nothing concrete as yet, not until I've performed the PM."

Katy motioned with her hand for Patti to hurry up. "Well, what is it?"

"Any time between eleven and eleven-thirty. May I ask why?"

Katy stared at the hedgerow, trying her hardest to remember what time she and Charlie had left Nadia's house. "Damn, I have a suspicion about a certain person. We were with her just before that time last night. If I recall, we left her gaff at around ten-fifteen, give or take a few minutes. Which means she had the time to get out here and kill him."

"Whoa! She? Who are we talking about here?"

"The daughter, Nadia Crawford. Something isn't sitting right with me. She acted strangely towards the men at the funeral. Finding her father like that and being covered in his blood, most SIOs would probably brush away my concerns but, she's a nurse; yes, instinct would kick in to save him, but surely, wouldn't she also take a step back, knowing it wouldn't be right for her to end up covered in his blood? Or am I guilty of overthinking things here?"

"Possibly. Put yourself in her shoes. Wouldn't you step up to the plate and help a loved one in dire need of your help?"

Katy sighed. "I guess. I can't explain why or what I'm feeling, Patti…" She spread a hand over her stomach. "It's here, something deep in my gut. Charlie and I paid her a visit last night to question her about Dale Peters' death. She had no alibi—she'd finished work at six, she could've easily followed him home and killed him. And now this. Obviously, I'll need to check if she stayed at home last night after we left or not. She did tell us she had to get up early, so I presumed she would've climbed into bed not long after we left."

"Maybe she did. What about coincidence, or doesn't that come into it?"

"You know I'm not really a believer in that. Okay, let's set that aside for now. Tell me how he died."

"He was clobbered is the best way to describe it, numerous times. Maybe the perpetrator carried out the attack over a few minutes, having a conversation in between, but the man suffered a fractured skull in several places, a broken jaw, plus dozens of other bones on his arms and legs. I will be noting this down as a frenzied attack, and you know what that means."

"I believe you're intimating that the perpetrator knew him well."

"That's often the case and would be my first port of call with any assumption I'm likely to make either before, during or after the post-mortem."

"Good to know. Shit, what a way to go out and in similar circumstances to the second victim. By that, I mean, out in the sticks. Why? I'm taking it that the perp knows where these guys live, follows them and attacks once there is no chance of someone witnessing the murders."

"I think you're right. The perp would definitely need to know where these guys live and the possible route they're likely to take home. Why would people pull over whilst driving, would you?"

"Nope, not a cat in hell's chance. What if the perp was coming in the opposite direction and blocked their path?"

"Plausible, I suppose. Who knows? I think the only person likely to tell us that would be the perp themselves."

Katy nodded and scanned the lit area. "Any DNA or evidence around?"

"Nothing so far."

"What type of weapon do you think they used, Patti?"

"Hard to say. My guess would be a heavy bar, possibly a crowbar. I'll be able to give a definitive answer after—"

"The PM," Katy finished off for her.

"How did you guess? Anyway, that's as much as I can tell you. Sorry for getting you out of bed early, I hope you can forgive me for that."

"Nothing to forgive. If you believe the crimes are linked, then yes, I should be here. I don't mind telling you, Patti, I don't know where to turn with this investigation. We're desperate for some form of evidence to show up, aren't we?"

"Too right. I have a suggestion to make, but you can tell me to butt out if you want."

"Go on, I'm all ears."

"Would it be worth putting a tail on your prime suspect?"

"I think I'm veering that way. At least if we tail her, we can pounce if we feel she's about to bump someone else off. Getting back to the victims: if she is guilty of killing them, we need to find out what her motive is. It would take a lot of angst to kill your own father, right?"

"Angst and a vast amount of courage. What age is she?"

"Around the twenty-eight mark, I believe."

"So, if, and it's a big if, she's the guilty party, something must have happened lately to have triggered such hatred to turn on her father after all this time, right?"

"Yep, you're not wrong. How the hell I'm supposed to work out what that trigger is, well, I fear it's beyond me. During the conversations we've had, she's not been as forthcoming as I would've preferred."

"What about relatives, can't you ask them?"

"There's only her sister, and she's up in Scotland." Katy chewed her lip and then clicked her thumb and finger together. "Her sister suggested that her father might have abused her. She left home at the age of sixteen, but Nadia chose to stay in the family home with her dad."

"Why? Did he abuse both girls or just one?"

Katy was enjoying this back and forth with Patti, who wasn't usually one for getting involved in the investigation side of things.

"I suppose I need to ask the right questions and see what trees I shake to get the answers."

"What about the mother?"

"Ah, yes, she died when the girls were both very young, three and four."

"Ouch, so he brought them up by himself? Not every father would do that, he was to be admired."

"I'm unsure about that. Maybe if he did abuse the kids, he didn't want the likes of anyone else hanging around. It's all supposition until the true facts emerge. Maybe I need to call her in for an interview at the station."

"That'll shit her up appropriately. Failing that, do as I suggested and put a tail on her for now. We'll hurry the PM and tests through for you on this and the other murders."

"Thanks, Patti, you're a goodun. I don't care what other officers say about you."

Patti slapped her arm. "Now, if you're finished, I'm going to tell you to piss off and let me get this man prepared for his journey to the mortuary."

"Speak soon, once you have the results back." Katy left the scene and removed her suit, dumping it in the awaiting black bag close to the cordon.

The drive to the station was performed on autopilot as Katy summarised things in her mind. Patti was spot on, it was imperative they put Nadia under surveillance, immediately. Her first job would be to arrange that then sort out a next of kin to break the news about Robin Hewitt. The clock on the dashboard said it was now nearing seven-thirty. Her stomach grumbled. She made a quick detour and drew up outside the café around the corner from the station. "A bacon roll to go, thanks."

The chubby woman behind the counter smiled and took the money from her. "No drink, love?"

"No, I'll get one at work."

"Very well. It'll be five minutes or so if you want to take a seat."

"Okay." Katy picked up a *Daily Mail* from the nearest table. She sat and whizzed through it, pausing to read the odd article of interest. The investigation into Bruce Crawford's death took up half a column on page fifteen. There was no blaming the police, and the fact that the paper had given the number for the station pleased her.

"Here you go, love. It's all ready for you. Help yourself to any sauce you might want."

"I'll take a sachet of ketchup and be on my way. I'm looking forward to this. See you again soon."

"Take care. Enjoy."

Katy slipped behind the steering wheel and pondered whether to eat the roll there and then but decided to continue on to the station instead.

She met up with Charlie in the car park.

"Hey, I'm going to tell AJ. What's up, isn't he feeding you enough?" Charlie laughed and pointed at the greasy paper bag Katy was holding.

"Ssh...actually, I've been at work for a while. Patti required my attendance at a murder scene, so I had to skip breakfast. For your cheek, you can buy your boss a cup of coffee."

"Ouch! Sorry you got called out, you should have given me a shout."

"Don't be silly. It's fine, no point in both of us walking around like the half-dead all day."

"Why you? Does Patti suspect the cases are connected?"

"Yep, so do I. You're never going to believe this...no, it can wait until the others arrive. My bacon roll, on the other hand, can't."

After bidding the grinning Mick a cheery good morning, they ascended the stairs to the incident room. They were the first to arrive. Charlie bought two cups of the Met's finest Colombian coffee—well, maybe that was stretching the truth a little too much.

"Come on, don't keep me dangling," Charlie said, handing her a cup of steaming coffee.

"All right. Take a seat. If you don't mind me speaking while I eat, I'll tell you. I'm glad it wasn't too gruesome. Saying that, it was bad enough."

"Go on," Charlie encouraged. She blew on her drink and then took a sip.

She went over the case and her thoughts as, one by one, the team arrived to join in the conversation.

"Did I hear right, you've been at another murder scene this morning, boss?" Patrick asked.

"You did. Thought I'd treat myself to a bacon roll as a reward." She half-grinned. "Seriously, we're going to need to start putting our heads together, thinking outside the box on this one, because up here," she tapped her temple, "none of this is making any bloody sense to me at all."

"We're doing our best with the clues we've been given," Karen replied. She seemed downbeat, as if all the fight in her had dissipated overnight.

"I know, that's the frustrating part, Karen. Listen up, I'm not blaming you guys, I'm just saying we're going to need to be clever about our thinking, see where that leads us."

Karen and the others present nodded. Katy glanced up at the clock. It was almost nine, and they were only waiting on Graham to arrive. It was unusual for him to be late.

He burst through the door with a minute to spare. "Shit! Sorry, boss, I had a flat tyre."

"Yeah, yeah. You're here now, get yourself a coffee and join us. We're discussing yet another murder that's been added to the investigation, Graham."

"Holy crap! Really? Where?"

"Take a seat. I was just about to fill everyone in." After she'd divulged the sequence of events that had led her to the scene a few hours earlier, she asked, "So, what are we missing, guys?"

A roomful of blank faces stared back at her.

"And we're sure all the crimes are linked?" Charlie tapped her pen on her pad.

"I'm in Patti's hands with the final one. She seems to believe they are, and I'm willing to take her word for that until she finds evidence to the contrary. Charlie and I will go break the news to the next of kin while you guys start to do the usual digging. See if Robin Hewitt is linked to the other men. If so, how and when? Karen, while I go over the post straining to be unleashed in my office, can you do an initial check on the victim for me, get his address, where he worked, that sort of thing?"

"On it now, boss."

"Good. Okay, guys, get thinking hard about this investigation. I'm not saying we've been guilty of slacking in the past week or so, but we need to prevent the body count from escalating further, got that?"

The team nodded and got down to business. Katy gathered her greasy bag and the remainder of her coffee and stepped into her office for the first time that morning. She surveyed the post littering her desk and blew out a relieved breath. *Not much, thank goodness.* She paused to open the window and took in a lungful of air which set her up for the chore ahead.

Twenty minutes later, and Charlie rapped her knuckles on the doorframe. "We've got his details, are you nearly finished?"

Katy held up a brown envelope. "Great timing, this is the last one. Let me deal with this, and we'll be off. One thing I forgot to mention was to get Hewitt's plate number, see if the ANPR or CCTV can pick him up sometime before his murder. And don't ask what time we should be looking at, cover the hours between ten and six, if you will."

"That could take forever to source."

"I'm aware of that. Your point is, Charlie?"

"Sorry, I was just putting it out there. I'll get the boys on it. It might take two of them to go through the amount of data in question."

"I was thinking along the same lines." She opened the final letter, and Charlie left her to it. She called her partner back. "Charlie, actually, this one concerns you."

Charlie entered the room. A deep frown had developed. "It does? Have I done something wrong?"

"Nope. Guess again."

"You tell me. I can't possibly think what it's concerning. Should I be worried about it?"

"Depends. It's notification of your place for the sergeant's exam."

Charlie collapsed into the chair in front of her. "Oh heck, my legs have gone all wobbly. When is it?"

"Two weeks. Are you ready for it?"

"Not really. Do you think I am?"

"Undoubtedly. You need to have faith in your abilities. You've slotted in well here, as if you've been on the force for years. You're dedicated and willing to learn. You've got this, Charlie. I don't want it to distract you from your work, though, you hear me?"

"Got it. Although I can't promise it's not going to be the elephant in the room at times. I think I'm up for the challenge."

"Think? It's a bit late for that, hon. The sooner you realise this is around the corner the better. Okay, I'm done here. Are those legs of yours working properly again?"

Charlie stood to test them. "They are."

"Then let's get on the road." Katy emptied her cup of coffee then wiped her mouth.

They stopped by Karen's desk on the way out to collect the latest victim's address and a brief rundown of his life, all that Karen had managed to find within the last thirty minutes anyway.

*T*he residential close was eerily quiet.

Katy switched off the engine. "Here we go." She puffed out her cheeks and hopped out of the vehicle.

They approached the small terraced house in a block of five, on the relatively new estate. The sound of nearby reversing beepers high-lighted that the area was still part of a building site. Katy rang the bell.

A few seconds later, a man in his thirties with a long fringe covering half his face opened the door. He had a tiny puppy in his arms. "Hello, can I help?"

"Nicky Wyatt?"

"Yes, that's right."

Katy held up her warrant card and introduced them. "May we come in and speak with you for a few moments?"

"Oh no, this is about Robin, isn't it? I've had a dreadful feeling all night that something's happened to him, I've barely slept."

Katy smiled faintly. "It would be better if we spoke inside, sir."

"You'd better come in. I'll just put Mr Pip in his basket. Go through to the lounge, I won't be long."

Katy and Charlie made themselves comfortable on the tan twin-seat leather sofa. Nicky joined them a few minutes later.

"Okay, give it to me straight, what's happened?"

"I'm afraid Robin Hewitt's body was found a few hours ago."

The man stared at them, no reaction whatsoever for a good few seconds until Katy's words sank in, then he placed his hands on either side of his face and screamed.

The noise was deafening in the snug room.

"Are you all right?" Katy asked, her nerves shattering into tiny pieces.

"All right? All right? I'll never be all right again. He was my life. I adored him. We were born to be together, and now…I'll never see his smiling face. Feel his arms around me to comfort me when I'm upset. Oh fuck, I think I'm going to pass out. I can't catch my breath." He clutched a hand to his chest.

"I'll fetch you a glass of water." Charlie raced out of the room and returned within seconds. She handed him the glass.

Nicky sipped his drink whilst shaking his head. "Bloody hell. How? Was it a car accident? I told him to get the thing serviced, it's been rattling for weeks. Would he listen to me? No, and now…"

"Please, try to calm down. It wasn't an accident. I'm sorry to have to inform you that Robin died in suspicious circumstances."

"Suspicious, in what way?"

"He was murdered."

Another scream flew out of the man's mouth. The cacophony battered Katy's ears. She resisted the temptation to cover them to block out the confounded racket. She'd met some off-the-wall reactions over the years, but this was the first time she's been faced with anything of this magnitude.

"No. Because he was *gay*? Is that it? Some fucker took an instant dislike to him because of his effeminate ways or possibly how he spoke and killed him for it? What kind of sick and disturbed world are we living in? People no longer have the freedom or choice in this life."

"You believe he was killed because he was gay?" Katy was floored by the suggestion.

Could that be the link between all the murders, that the other men were gay? But surely not, Dale Peters was married.

"Why not? Most people can't accept it when people's preferences change."

"I'm sorry, I don't understand what you're saying. Can you enlighten us?"

He sighed and let out a shuddering breath. "He used to be married…to a woman until we met. Our love was strong from the moment we first laid eyes on each other."

"Oh, I see. How long was he married?"

"About twenty years, maybe longer, I wasn't that interested in what went on in his life before I came along. We had a secure, loving relationship."

"But he was married when he started seeing you?"

"Yes, what does that have to do with anything? No, you don't think that bitch knocked him off, do you?"

"Bitch? Are you possibly referring to the woman who shared his life with him all those years?"

"Yeah, whatever you want to call it. She was livid when he asked her to set him free."

Katy inclined her head. "For a divorce, you mean?"

"Yes. That's right. She threatened all sorts."

"Do you have her name and address handy?"

"Oh yes, as if I'm likely to forget that."

"Did they have any children together?" Katy asked as Nicky searched through the coffee table drawer for something.

"No. She couldn't have them. They even tried IVF when they were a few years younger. All that money wasted because each month her body rejected the eggs."

Katy neither liked nor appreciated the way Nicky was portraying the ex-wife. She felt he was being unfairly harsher than was necessary. "That's a shame. Are you telling me that she lashed out and blatantly threatened you guys?"

"Not in so many words, but there was no doubting her disgust. I wouldn't put it past her to have a hand in this. Here you go, do you want to copy it?"

Charlie took the notebook from him, jotted down the information and handed it back to him. "Thanks, I think I've deciphered it correctly."

Nicky tutted. "Want me to read it out to you?"

"If you wouldn't mind, just to be on the safe side," Charlie replied.

"Laila Hewitt, forty-seven Forrester Road, Whitechapel. She got the house, and he walked away with nothing. He did all that to be with me. Why? Because we loved each other."

"He took nothing, no furniture?"

"That's right. I advised him not to take anything, to let her have it all because of the damn fuss she was kicking up about him coming out."

"You thought her reaction to the situation was over the top?"

"I should say so. She saw us holding hands in a restaurant once, stormed up to us, slapped him around the face and spat in his dinner, she was so incensed. He had to restrain me. I wanted to pull her fucking hair out and shove her capped teeth down her throat. Why are people always so bitter come the end of their relationships? Why can't they just remember the good times and move on?"

"Twenty-odd years to be married to someone and not realise they're gay…it kind of blows the mind. She would've been left doubting her abilities as a woman. I'm only guessing that's what would have been running through her mind, not having been in the situation myself, of course."

"These things happen, people need to learn to adjust and let the person go. There's no point hanging on to someone who doesn't want to be around, is there?"

"True enough. Has Laila been in touch with either of you lately?"

"No. We haven't heard from her in a few months, not since the decree absolute came through. She rang and shouted down the phone, 'Good riddance!' It was pretty clear she wouldn't want anything more to do with Robin. He told me that was a relief, as remaining friends with her after they'd been intimate all those years would have been a nightmare for him."

"I see. Does she work? Have anything to occupy her mind now?"

"Not sure on the latter, but no, she's never worked a day in her life."

"That must've been hard on Robin, to be the sole provider in the house."

"Yep, my thoughts exactly. I pay my way around here. I work full-time, you've caught me on my day off today. I wouldn't have it any other way. I love my independence. Not her, that's why she begged him to stay, even after he came out to her. She pleaded with him to make it work with her."

"She sounded desperate."

"My sentiment exactly. And desperate women are prone to doing desperate things, right?"

"Occasionally. I'd rather not cast aspersions at this stage. We'll need to speak with her to get her side of things first."

He stared and narrowed his eyes. "Typical, women sticking together. Don't take my word for it, will you?"

"DC Simpkins has noted everything down in her notebook. If we have to refer back to it during our conversation with her, we will. Have either you or Robin encountered any other problems recently?"

"No. We're careful who we mix with. The only time Robin has been out of my sight was when he attended his old friend's funeral last week."

Katy's interest soared. "Funeral? The name of the person who died was?"

"Bruce Crawford."

"And they were close, were they?"

"Many years back. They'd lost contact with each other over the years, and he was surprised when he'd received the call from Bruce Crawford's daughter saying her father was being buried, inviting him to attend."

"Nadia?"

"I think that was her name. Why? What does this have to do with Robin's death?"

"It might be nothing; however, Robin's death is the third case we've stumbled across where the victims all knew each other."

"No! What are you saying?"

"That something might have gone on in the men's history that we need to get to the bottom of. Did Robin ever speak about anything?"

"No, nothing. We were happy, content to be with each other. We focused on the good things in life instead of anything bad."

"What was his reaction to Bruce's death? Did you notice a change in him at all?"

His gaze drifted to the photo on the dresser by the far wall and he sighed. "I suppose looking back on it, he did seem a little subdued. I didn't press him, put it down to him mourning an old friend and a close friendship, nothing more."

"I see. What about a Dale Peters, did he ever mention him?"

He leaned a hand against his face and thought. "I don't think so, it's not a name I recognise, sorry. Why do you ask?"

"He's the other victim I mentioned, another gentleman whose murder we're trying to solve at this time."

"And you think there's a connection?"

"Yes, at least that's our understanding. How they knew each other is the one thing we've yet to figure out."

He shrugged. "Are you suggesting they were more than just friends who went out socialising together, is that it?"

Katy shrugged back. "It's all a bit foggy, and we need to obtain a clearer image if we're going to solve the cases."

"Hadn't you better get out there? Aren't you wasting time being here?"

"I wouldn't call it a waste of time, Nicky. It was our job to inform you of your partner's death, which we've done. Are you sure there's nothing in Robin's past that he has revealed to you that you think would help our investigation?"

"Nope. I'd definitely be considering Laila." He twisted a finger into his temple. "She's always been a bit unhinged in my eyes. Worth doing an in-depth into her life."

"We'll definitely be doing that in the next day or two."

"You haven't told me how he died? I can take it, you know, the truth."

"He was beaten with something heavy. Anything more than that, I can't tell you, not until the post-mortem has been performed, which should take place today, all being well."

He visibly shuddered and sucked in a breath. "Does he have to be cut open? Can't they examine him without slicing him up?"

"The pathologist has to do it, I'm afraid. Any suspicious deaths need to be investigated thoroughly."

"Will I be able to see him?"

"Once the PM is out of the way, the pathologist's department will ring you to make all the necessary arrangements for you to see him. Again, I'm so sorry for your loss."

"We'd made plans to get married next year. We were in the process of saving up to fly out to Las Vegas. Both of us have always wanted Elvis to marry us." He held his head in his hands and sobbed.

"I'm so sorry. Is there someone you'd like me to call to come and be with you?"

"No, I'm not really one to air my feelings in public. I'll get through this; it might take me a while. He was a wonderful man. So giving with his time, his patience was second to none, and his love knew no bounds. I shall miss him. Mr Pip and I will get through this together, though. We're tough, resilient buggers. I think we are, yes, we are, we will survive. I'm sure we will. Is there anything else you need to ask?"

"Only what Robin's job was."

"He was a local actor at the theatre. He also did voice-over work at one of the studios nearby. Do you want me to write down the addresses for you? Are you thinking it could be someone who worked at either of those places who might have killed him?"

"It's better to be armed with the facts. We'll need to have a word with his colleagues. Did he work yesterday?"

"Yes, he was at the voice-over studio until around ten last night. That's a regular job. He's been doing the same routine for months now, if that helps."

"It does. When he didn't come home last night, weren't you worried about him?"

"Of course I was. I rang a few of his colleagues, the ones I had the numbers for. They all told me they hadn't seen him. Sometimes he went to the studio alone, told me he could get more work done that way. Actually, now and then he chose to work through the night if things were flowing well for him."

"Without notifying you?"

"No, that was unusual, which is why I kept ringing him. It wasn't until I saw you standing on my doorstep that the penny dropped, why I hadn't been able to contact him."

Katy and Charlie stood.

Nicky did the same, walked out of the room and showed them to the door. "Please promise me you won't give up searching for this person. You hear of so many cases remaining unsolved these days. I would hate for Robin to become one of those statistics."

"You have my word that we're going to do our very best. Here's a card. If you hear of anything we should know about, give me a call."

"I will. Thank you."

Katy smiled and made her way back to the car. "What do you think about that revelation?" She slotted the key into the ignition. "Put the wife's postcode into the satnav before giving me your answer."

Charlie flipped open her notebook and punched in the code. "Twenty-three minutes. Enough time for us to have a conversation before we get there."

"I like your thinking. Go on, you first."

"Why would he come out after all those years?"

"Good question. One that has always flummoxed me. Maybe the right person hadn't come along. Do you think the wife could be the killer?"

Charlie snorted. "Her and dozens of others by the sounds of it. The honest answer is, I don't suppose we'll have an inkling until we sit down and speak to her. I wonder what her reaction is going to be when we show up at her door."

"It could be a situation of her going down the fight or flight route, so be prepared—that is assuming she has something to hide. I have my doubts. This whole investigation is driving me batty. One minute I think it's the daughter, the next I don't think she could possibly be behind the murders, and now we've got another potential candidate. Would a woman wronged the way she's been, be tempted to kill her ex, just for the sake of it?"

"Pride comes into it, I suppose. I don't really know enough about the subject to feel that I can offer a suitable answer. Who knows what goes through a woman's mind when the person she has loved for over twenty years tells her they're leaving her for someone of the opposite gender? Would you know how to react if AJ said the same?"

"Blimey, I really wouldn't want to put myself in that position. How would you feel if Brandon came home and announced something similar?"

"That's just it, I don't think either of us could speculate unless we were thrust into that dilemma. I can't imagine any woman reacting calmly, can you?"

"But then, I'm not going to mention names, but I can think of a few high-profile celebrities who have shocked the nation in the past few years by doing just that and their wives have stuck by them. Is it a case of the women settling into a new life with their men? I believe the celebrities I'm thinking about, didn't actually go off with someone of the same sex, they've simply come out and admitted they're gay. Who knows what the future holds for either party? Has the man 'come out' in the hope that the woman would go on to find true love with another man? It's all so confusing to know what to think."

Charlie glanced out of the window at the passing shops. "It's definitely not a situation I would relish finding myself in, I can categorically say that."

"I totally get that. I could see some women spiralling out of control. Where that could possibly lead is anybody's guess. Maybe we should stop speculating until we meet the woman in person and see how she appears to be coping. I wonder if she's found a job yet. She'd need to get one, she can't support herself on thin air. Which could be another tick for her exacting her revenge."

Charlie turned her attention to the road ahead again. "Possibly. Like you say, to speculate without ever laying eyes on the woman could be foolish and jeopardise the investigation."

"Yep, what say we stop off for a coffee before we head over there? I can think of a lovely coffee shop en route, only a few miles away."

Charlie chuckled. "If I know you, the coffee will need to be accompanied by a cake or pastry."

"Maybe. Are you up for it?"

"Can I remind you that you stuffed a bacon roll down your neck barely an hour ago?"

Katy faced her and grinned. "I did, didn't I? Naughty me. I need at least two cups of coffee to get me going in the morning, and so far, I've only had the one. That's my excuse and I'm sticking to it."

"You're impossible. Go on then, if we must."

*A*fter reviving themselves with a much-needed cup of coffee and resisting the tempting array of cakes on offer, they continued on their journey over to Laila Hewitt's house, presuming she hadn't ditched her married name by now after being cast aside the way she had.

The semi-detached red-brick house had a welcoming front garden which was a riot of colour. Bedding plants filled every possible gap in between the more permanent shrubs on either side of the path. Charlie beat Katy to ring the bell this time.

The door opened to reveal a woman in her late forties to early fifties resembling Cherie Blair, the former Prime Minister's wife. Her petite frame was clad in a rich velvet green leisure suit.

Katy displayed her warrant card. "Laila Hewitt, I'm DI Katy Foster, and this is my partner, DC Charlie Simpkins. Do you have a free moment to speak with us?"

"Oh my. The police? What on earth could you want with me?" The rosy colour quickly left her cheeks.

"Would it be possible to come inside? It might be better."

"Better? For whom? I have extremely nosey neighbours, Inspector, I'll be the talk of the street if I let you in. No, say what you have to say here, where my neighbours can see you."

Katy hadn't been expecting her to respond in that way. She cleared her throat and asked, "Very well. May I ask if you've heard from your ex-husband recently?"

"No. Why should I hear from him? He's made his bed…so to speak."

Katy nodded. "We're aware there might be some animosity between you."

"Understatement of the decade. I hate the bastard for what he put me through. The humiliation. The shame only a man without love in his heart could bestow upon someone —their wife, should I say."

"It must have been very difficult for you to deal with. Please, I have some news and I'd rather not tell you while standing on your doorstep."

Finally relenting, she stepped aside and allowed them to enter. She pointed into the hallway. "First room on the right. Excuse the mess, I was just going through my photo albums and getting rid of anything pertaining to my former husband. It's taken me months to pluck up the courage to get around to tackling the task."

"Fair enough. We're not here to judge you on your housekeeping standards," Katy replied.

She swept past Laila and into the room. It was littered with thousands of pictures. No wonder the woman had taken the news about their split badly. She had cherished the man she was once married to for over twenty years. She and AJ didn't have many photos of them as a couple; they did have a few of them with Georgie, however. But nothing compared to this display.

Laila grabbed a pile of photos which had been torn up into pieces and shoved them into a black sack. "Take a seat, won't you?"

Katy and Charlie did as instructed and sat on the dark-brown velour sofa, beyond the mess on the floor.

"Thanks. Is it all right if I call you Laila?"

"Why shouldn't it be? It's my name. I'm still waiting to receive the go-ahead from my solicitor to dump my married name, which is taking forever to sort out. Until then, I'm stuck with it. I detest it, though. Can't wait to return to Watkins, my maiden name."

"I can understand your reasoning behind that."

"I'm not one for idle chitchat, Inspector. You mentioned you had some news for me, what is it?"

"It's with regret I have to inform you that your ex-husband has died."

Laila flopped into the easy chair behind her and stared at Katy as if a dozen venomous snakes had slithered out of her mouth. "What?" she whispered, finally recovering her voice.

"He was killed and found early this morning."

Her head moved from side to side in slow motion. "But…but, why tell me? We haven't had anything to do with each other for over six months."

"We've just come from the home he shared with Nicky and we had a few unanswered questions. He suggested we trace you and run them past you."

"He did? What sort of questions? Don't tell me you think I had something to do with his death?"

"No, not at this point anyway. We believe Robin's death is linked to two other murders in the area and wondered if you could shed any light on why they might have occurred."

Her head shook harder and faster this time. "What are you getting at? Linked how? Who were the other victims?"

"Bruce Crawford and Dale Peters. I can tell by the look on your face that you recognise the names. Can you tell me where from?"

"I do. They all used to be friends. Did I hear you right? All three of them are dead?" Confusion settled into her features, and she placed a hand against her cheek.

"I'm afraid so, yes. Nicky didn't appear to know much about their friendship and pointed us in your direction." Katy noted the woman flinched every time she mentioned her ex's lover's name. She shouldn't have been surprised.

"Why should he? He's a relative newcomer in Robin's life, whereas I spent over twenty years with the man."

"Can you enlighten us regarding their friendship?"

"I can try. At one time they used to be very close. Always met round at Bruce's house. How his wife put up with them turning up on her doorstep every week I'll never know, God rest her soul."

"Did you know the other spouses or girlfriends? Did you perhaps meet up as a group?"

"Only at weddings or funerals. As for socialising together, no, only the men did that. It didn't bother me, I preferred to spend time on my own rather than every waking moment with him and his friends anyway. They weren't really my type, if you know what I mean?"

"I see. Did their friendship dwindle after a while, is that what you're telling us?"

"I suppose it did. I asked Robin on numerous occasions why they'd stopped socialising, and he snapped at me regularly when I pushed him. The final time he shouted at me, told me never to raise the subject again, which I didn't."

"How strange, and you have no inkling what it could have been about?"

"None. The more I pushed, the more he retreated until the day he bit my head off. I didn't appreciate him speaking to me like that. All I was doing was trying to find out why he no longer wanted to speak to either of them."

"They cut off all contact?"

"Yes." She sniffled and reached for a tissue from the packet sitting alongside the photos. "Oh God, I can't believe he's gone. What was I thinking? I had every intention of destroying all these today. What if I'd done that and you showed up half an hour later to tell me the news? I would have been devastated. Deep down he was a good man, I know that now. My reaction, the pure hatred I've felt for him since…you know, since he revealed he was going off with another fella, while it was probably expected, I realise now how unacceptable it was. I regret the way I've treated him the past six months or so. I can never take back the harsh words…I can't believe he's no longer with us. Who did this, do you know?"

"No. We believe it's probably linked to something that happened back when they were a group. By what you've just told us, it definitely backs up our assumption. Please, can you try to remember, see if anything comes to mind?"

She sat there quietly for several minutes, contemplating Katy's plea, and then disappointedly shook her head. "I'm sorry, nothing."

"You mentioned the wife's death. Do you know what the cause was?"

"No, apparently Bruce said that she'd died of complications in her sleep."

"Can you remember what year that was?"

"Gosh, now you're testing me. Around ninety-five, possibly ninety-six. What am I saying? It might even have been a year or two either side. I can't honestly remember."

"Didn't you go to the funeral?"

"No. Neither of us were asked to attend."

"How bizarre. You don't think that decision was the cause of their friendship ending, do you?"

Laila stared at the corner of the room for a second or two. "Possibly, if I was positive about the year of her death, maybe I could answer that for you."

"It's fine. We'll look it up when we get back, don't worry."

"They had two girls I seem to recall, maybe you could ask them."

"I intend to, we've met both of them."

"How are they coping with the loss of their father? Can I ask how he died? I always figured he was the type to live forever, if you get my meaning?"

"I think so. His daughter found him after a suspected burglary."

"Oh my, that's terrible. She must have been traumatised?"

"She wasn't in good spirits, let's say that. Did you ever have children, Laila?"

"No, which I see as a blessing in disguise, considering how our marriage ended."

"During your marriage, did any situation arise that may have been a cause of concern for Robin?"

"I don't understand what you're getting at."

"Did he possibly fall out with anyone who might have threatened him?"

"No, nothing like that. My husband was a lover not a fighter. Good grief, did I really say that out loud?"

Katy smiled and nodded. "It's okay, I appreciate the position you're in. You still loved him right up until the end, didn't you?"

"Yes." Tears emerged and trickled onto her cheeks. "You don't spend most of your adult life with someone and stop loving them just because they suddenly announced they're gay. It's not that I'm bitter, far from it. If anything, I feel ashamed, guilty even that I was unable to read the signs when they were clearly evident throughout our marriage. I took his gentle nature at face value when all along he had an affinity to me. Does that make sense? It does in my head."

"I think so. Please, try not to get upset. Life gets in the way for all of us at times. You're definitely not the first woman this has ever happened to, and I doubt you'll be the last either. I wouldn't take it personally. Maybe set it aside as one of life's more dubious lessons and attempt to get over it. You're far too young to spend it on your own."

"I know. I keep telling myself that, but the reality is, I know deep down I'll never be able to trust another man, not intimately. He's left me with very little self-worth. I gave him everything, opened myself up to him, and that's how he repaid me. By using me as a cover for his warped sexuality. God, I swore I'd never get this worked up over him again, and now, he's gone, leaving me with so many unanswered questions which I hoped, over time, he might have had the courage to answer."

Warped sexuality? "Have you sought counselling?"

"No. I'm fine. Who am I kidding? I'm a survivor. I'll get through this. In fact, I was coping remarkably well until you showed up on my doorstep."

Katy shook her head. "I'm sorry. Bad timing, but an essential visit nonetheless. Is there anything else about Robin's relationship with the other men that you can think of?"

"No. Please, you're going to have to leave this with me. The news of Robin's death isn't allowing me to think straight."

"Okay. Would it be all right if I left you my card?"

"Of course, please do. I'll do my very best to try and revisit the memories I've locked away and come up with some answers for you."

"We appreciate your help under these trying circumstances, Laila. We'll let you get on with your day." Katy glanced down at the photos spread over the floor.

Laila sighed. "I suppose I'd better hang on to a few of these now. I'll show you out. Sorry I couldn't be much help."

"Nonsense, just give us a call if your mind unleashes anything worthwhile."

"I will. I promise."

10

———————

The man was the last to leave. He locked up the front doors to the supermarket and raced around the side of the building to the car park at the rear to collect his car. Suddenly, he found himself bathed in the glare of full-beam headlights, his chance to react lost when someone ran at him and knocked him to the ground.

"What the fuck are you doing?"

Another whack to the head with the metal bar, and he almost lost consciousness, hovering on the brink. He froze and looked up at his assailant. His mouth hung open for a few seconds, and then he whispered, "It's you? But…"

"How?" his attacker finished off for him.

"Yes, how?"

The blows came then, heavier with each one until the assailant's arms grew tired and he lay unconscious on the tarmac.

❧

"Damn, it was too quick. I despise you. For what you did back then, you're despicable beyond words."

Walking back to the car, the attacker refused to glance at Ellis Bird.

The engine was already running. Foot on the accelerator, the car drew away, not bothering to go around the obstruction. Instead, the car rocked from side to side as the wheels connected with the man's body.

Even if he wasn't dead before, his breath will have left his body now.

Screeching out of the car park and into the flow of traffic, it was a long time before the killer let out the stale breath burning their lungs.

"I did it. Another one down. The list is getting shorter."

The final blow would be dealt tomorrow, if everything went according to plan in the meantime.

No remorse…never feel remorse, not when the repayment is so sweet.

11

*K*aty didn't make it home at a reasonable hour even that night, work and the clues they were chasing saw to that.

Damn this killer, they're definitely keeping me on my bloody toes.

Patti greeted her with as much enthusiasm as she felt for attending a murder scene at eleven o'clock at night. "Hi, did you make it home?"

"Nope, did you?" Katy asked.

"I wish. I was finishing up a PM when I got the call about this one. Tell me you're getting closer to picking this bastard up. I'm not sure how long I can last without seeing my comfy bed."

"Why don't you delegate? You work too hard. Surely there are other pathologists who could take your place, aren't there?"

"Nope, we're short-staffed. Anyway, if you want something done the right way, it's better to do it yourself rather than rely on someone else's inept attempt to accurately portray what happened."

"Fair enough. Care to fill us in?"

Katy and Charlie shuffled forward, their protective suits and shoes rustling in the slight breeze, to get a closer look at the victim highlighted under the temporary spotlights the SOCO team had erected at regular intervals around the corpse.

"The victim is apparently the manager of the supermarket. You'll be pleased to know we have a witness to this one, ladies."

"Well, that's good news. Where are they?" Katy scanned the area.

Patti pointed to a vehicle with its interior light on, beyond the car park in a side street. "An older gentleman, he's pretty shaken up."

"I can imagine. Does he know the vic?"

"Not sure. What, you want me to do your job for you?"

"All right, don't have a pop at me. Go on, what about the vic, how did he die?" Katy peered closer at the body. "No, that's not tyre marks over his face?"

"It is. There are several other injuries. Again, I'm linking this one to the previous victim if only due to the similar weapon being used. My take is that he was beaten with a metal bar and then run over to ensure he was dead."

"Jesus. This perp definitely isn't keen on leaving any loose ends, like keeping one of them alive, right?"

"Yep, the same thought ran through my frazzled mind. They're keen to make sure no one survives the attack."

"So definitely premeditated. None of the other victims had been burgled, so each of the attacks had been thought through, I'd say," Katy suggested.

"You have an ID for him?" Charlie asked.

"Yep, his name is Ellis Bird and his address is on his driving licence if you want to make a note of it, Charlie, it's in the evidence bag over there."

"Thanks, I'll get it." Charlie stepped away.

Patti and Katy crouched beside the corpse. Patti said, "The fear was still showing in his eyes when I arrived. The first thing I did was to close them."

"Shame they didn't reflect who the bloody murderer was. This investigation frigging stinks."

"Maybe having a witness this time around will give you the impetus you need to move forward."

"Why allow someone to see them? The killer has been extra vigilant up until now, so why change?"

"Maybe because we're in the middle of a high street this time. Perhaps the killer thought this would be the ideal spot to kill him if he was aware of where he lives. I don't know the area this particular victim lives in, it could be built up compared to the previous two vics."

Katy rubbed her chin. "You could have a valid point." Charlie reappeared and showed Katy the address. "I know it, and yes, Patti, you're right, it's too built up. Killing him here would've likely been their only option, except they hadn't bargained on there being a witness."

"Or CCTV footage from the security cameras at the rear of the building."

"Crap, I hadn't noticed," Katy said. "We'll get those sorted ASAP first thing in the morning, remind me, Charlie, will you?"

"I'll arrange to get the footage myself, how's that, boss?"

"Good, good. Okay, I'd better have a word with the witness, get his take on things and send him on his way. I'll be back soon." Katy walked in the direction of the parked vehicle.

The driver was staring at her with every step she took towards him.

"You do that. I'll finish up here and get the vic settled in the fridge overnight, ready to start the PM in the morning. There's no way I'm doing it tonight, not after the day I've had."

"About time you put your foot down, Patti," Katy bellowed over her shoulder.

The man opened his car door and hopped out from behind the steering wheel.

Katy smiled. "Hello, sir. I'm DI Katy Foster, the SIO on the investigation. Would you mind telling me what you saw? As it's rather late, we'll arrange to take a proper statement from you in the next day or two, if that's okay with you?"

"I'm Paul Somers. I don't mind either way. Yes, okay. Right, well, I'd nipped in the supermarket to get a bottle of wine. They'd run out of their usual quality brand, and stocks were quite low, therefore, I decided to nip around the corner to the off-licence. I bought a similar grape variety and was just on my way back when a car came tearing out of the car park. Almost mowed me down in the driver's haste to get out of here. I was livid. Raised my fist at the bastard, sorry, to the thug, but they refused to stop. I was grateful they drove off when I came around the corner and saw him…lying there."

"The victim?"

"Yes. I know first aid but decided to hold back. I did touch his neck to see if there was a pulse, no such luck. I got on the phone to the operator right away, called nine-nine-nine and requested the police, apprised the operator of the situation. The woman asked if I required an ambulance as well. I made the call not to have one. It was obvious he'd gone. Why would anyone do something like that to another human being? The car which left in a hurry obviously did it on purpose, right? No one knocks someone over like that and leaves the scene, do they?"

"Unfortunately, hit-and-runs happen all too often for my liking. Did you get a good look at the vehicle, sir?"

"Yeah, and the driver, although I won't be able to give you much there, as they were wearing one of those vile hoodies. The car was a red VW, one of the sporty versions."

Katy jotted the information down and hesitated, apprehension spiking whether she dare ask the next question on her tongue. "And the registration number?"

He held up a finger and dipped into his car. He emerged holding up an old envelope. "You're in luck. I don't usually have a pen and paper on me. It just so happens I had a list with me tonight while I went shopping."

He handed the paper over, and again she wrote down the information, her adrenaline shoving aside the apprehension she'd felt a moment earlier.

"That's brilliant. If I can take down your address."

He reeled it off. "Any assistance I can give, just shout. We need to rid the streets of these maniacs, there are far too many of them these days. If it's not knife crimes…sorry, you don't need me telling you that, I'm sure you're aware of the crimes we have to put up with in this area."

Katy smiled. "Sadly, all too well. I have to action this information swiftly if we're going to catch the person responsible, sir. I can't thank you enough for being super observant. We'll be in touch soon."

"My pleasure. I'll be on my way then."

Katy called the station as she darted back to the crime scene. "Yes, I need to get a bulletin out. All vehicles to be on the lookout for a red VW with this registration number…" She read out the details to the woman on control. "I need the ANPR cameras checked as well. My partner and I are on our way back to the station now."

"Leave it with me, Inspector Foster. I'll get this actioned ASAP."

"Keep me informed, as and when you find anything." Katy ended the call and watched Paul Somers leave the area. "I wish there were more diligent people like him around, it would make our lives a lot easier. He got the plate number. I've asked control to get onto it now. Charlie, you and I should make a move. I think we might have a long night ahead of us."

"I'm up for it. I've already rung Brandon to pre-warn him not to expect me before midnight."

"I've got to break the bad news to AJ yet. Can't say I'm relishing the prospect. But needs must as they say. We need to catch this bastard, and soon. Tonight would be ideal."

"What are you hanging around here for then?" Patti asked. "Shoo…let me get on with my work. Judging by the clouds gathering, I think we're going to get a downpour soon enough. They predicted a bout of thunderstorms at the beginning of the week, but they haven't materialised as yet. It'll be just my luck the heavens open tonight."

"Less chatter and more work then would be my advice." Katy winked at the pathologist.

"All right, I'm on it now. Good luck, keep me informed if you find the suspect."

"Don't worry, you'll be at the top of the list."

Katy and Charlie tore off their protective gear and ran back to the car, dumping the suits in a sack close to Patti's van.

"Things are definitely looking up for us, Charlie."

"Good, it's about time."

Katy decided to text AJ to break the news to him. A response came back within seconds: *Stay safe. I love you.*

She sent three love hearts and an *I love you* in return.

*K*aty wasn't looking forward to telling yet another victim's family about their loved one's passing, but here she was, standing outside the family home, jiggling from foot to foot while she waited for someone to open the door.

It took a while for the woman to appear. She had her hair wrapped in a towel, her dressing gown pulled tightly around her. "Hello, can I help?"

"So sorry to disturb you, Mrs Bird." Katy showed the woman her ID. "Would it be possible to come in and speak with you?"

"Oh my, it's not my husband, is it? Ellis is late home, and I've tried calling him several times but received no response. I thought a bath would help me to relax. I was getting myself in a right state."

"Yes, it's concerning your husband."

She clutched a hand to her chest and staggered back into the hallway, allowing them access. Charlie closed the door behind them, and they followed the shocked woman into the first room on the left. The lounge was decorated in muted brown and creams. Large geometric pattern curtains covered the two windows. Mrs Bird took a seat by the fireplace and motioned for Katy and Charlie to sit on the sofa.

"Please don't tell me something dreadful has happened to him. I couldn't bear you telling me that. We've had such a dreadful few months. Both our fathers have died recently, and the loss has been horrendous to deal with."

Katy swallowed down the lump that had emerged in her larynx. "I'm sorry, it is bad news, I'm afraid. This evening, your husband's body was found lying in the car park at the rear of the supermarket."

The woman listened. Her mouth dropped open, and she shook her head. "No, don't tell me that. Not Ellis. Not my baby. He can't be gone, I need him." She covered her face with her hands.

"Charlie, can you make Mrs Bird a cup of tea?"

Her partner rose and tore out of the room, Katy suspected out of relief. She wished she could do the same.

"I'm sorry for breaking down, he's my everything."

"Is there someone else in the house or someone you'd like me to call to come and be with you?"

"No, there's only us here now. The children have both left home, they have their own families. How am I going to break the news to them? They both adore their father."

"Would you like me to call one of them, would that help?"

"No. I'll do it." She reached for the mobile sitting on the small octagonal table beside her chair and scrolled through it. "Gemma, sorry to wake you, love...yes, I know it's late...I've got the police here...it's your father...something dreadful has happened...can you come and be with me? I quite understand if you don't want to...okay, I'll see you then. Goodbye, sweetheart." Amy ended the call. "She's going to contact her sister. They both live around the corner. If they lived farther away then I wouldn't have told her over the phone for fear of either of them crashing. Sorry, I'm wittering on. My mind is racing ahead. He was found, was it a heart attack? I thought he seemed a little peaky a few days ago, but that wore off. He assured me he was fine and that he didn't want to visit the doctor. Now he's dead. Why didn't he listen to me? Stubborn bloody man."

Charlie returned and placed a mug on the table next to Mrs Bird. "There you go, I've made it nice and sweet to ease the shock."

"Thank you, dear, that's most kind of you."

Katy struggled to find the words to tell the woman the truth without causing her further distress. "No, it wasn't his heart, at least not initially. Your husband was attacked, which led to him being murdered. I'm sorry, I know that's not what you want to hear."

Mrs Bird stared blankly at her, her hands clenching and unclenching in her lap. A noise sounded in the hallway. Her gaze drifted to the door, and two young women entered the room. They hugged their mother, sobbing and crying in disbelief.

Amy Bird appeared to gather strength from her daughters' appearance. "There, there, loves. Everything is going to be all right. Come, sit with me. The inspector was just about to tell me what happened to your father."

The three of them squeezed onto the easy chair, Amy taking her seat while her two dumbstruck daughters balanced on either arm.

Katy smiled tautly at the two daughters. "I'm so sorry to have to share this news with you all this evening."

"What happened? Is he going to be all right?" one of the newcomers barked.

Her mother patted her knee. "No, sweetheart, he's gone."

"Gone? As in, dead?"

Their mother nodded. "Yes, let's hear the inspector out, Gemma, she's trying to do her job."

"I need to know how he went," Gemma replied. She placed an arm around her mother's shoulders.

"Your father was found in the car park behind the shop," Katy said. "The pathologist is still at the scene. I won't be able to share her findings with you just yet, not until a post-mortem has been carried out."

Gemma shrugged. "What have you told us except that he's dead? Don't you think we have a right to know?"

"Of course you do." Katy sighed. "I appreciate how difficult this is for you all. What I can tell you is that we're dealing with several other suspicious deaths in the area which have occurred in the past week to ten days."

"Suspicious in what way?" the other daughter asked.

"All the men were murdered, we're presuming by the same suspect."

"What?" Gemma leapt to her feet and crossed the room to stand in front of Katy and Charlie. "You're telling us he was murdered? How? Why? Why him? What are you doing about it? Shouldn't you be out there trying to find his killer instead of being here with us?"

"Gemma, please, sit down," Amy said, her tone stern but gentle.

"No, Mum, I want answers and I don't hear any forthcoming so far." She faced Katy again and, hands jabbing at her hips, she demanded, "Well?"

"Gemma, we're doing our best. Since the first murder occurred, our investigation has been at full pelt, I promise you."

"And the murderer has been allowed to commit yet more murders. To rob families of their loved ones, why? Because you're inept at your job, is that it?"

"Gemma, either you apologise for your outburst or I'll send you home," her mother chastised.

"Send me home, Mother? I'm not bloody ten."

"Then stop acting as if you are and give the officers some room. You're intimidating them and upsetting me further in the process. Show some respect, I've just lost my husband."

"And I've just lost my *father*. A man I loved dearly and who I'll miss until God takes me from this earth. Why? Why him? I keep asking the question but I'm not receiving any plausible answers. Why not?"

Her sister left her seat and guided Gemma back to their mother's side. They both sat heavily once more.

"Please, while I understand the anger and trauma you're experiencing right now, I can assure you, my team and I have all been working flat out on this investigation this week." Katy wanted to add that she'd barely seen her own family since the first murder had happened. Her frustration level kicked up a notch.

"And do you have anyone in mind?" Gemma's eyes narrowed during her question.

"Not yet. That's not quite true, we have a possible suspect in mind. The problem is, we've been unable to act upon our suspicions because the suspect's alibis have always checked out."

"Alibis?" Amy queried.

"Yes, for when the incidents occurred. The pathologist can always give us a rough timeline. You can help us gather more information to add to the mix, if you're willing to answer our questions this evening."

"About what?" Amy asked.

"Yeah, about what?" Gemma repeated.

"Can you tell us if your husband has mentioned someone possibly following him lately?"

"No, he never mentioned anything like that. Had he mentioned it, I would've told him to get in touch with the police. Are you telling us you believe someone was possibly stalking him?"

"Maybe. It's not something we're willing to rule out yet. A nugget of information that has come to our attention this week is that all victims are linked."

"Linked how?" Gemma was quick to jump in.

"We believe they all knew each other. We have suspicions that something possibly happened in their past that has come back to haunt them now. Can you think of anything in your husband's past that could be the catalyst to all this?"

Amy tucked the end of the towel back around her neck to secure it in place. "No, I can't think of anything. Maybe if you told me who the other victims are that would jog my memory."

Gemma glared at Katy and demanded, "Are you saying our dad was guilty of being part of something illegal?"

"I'm not saying anything of the sort, Gemma. The other victims are Bruce Crawford, Dale Peters and Robin Hewitt. Do any of those names ring a bell with you, Amy?"

Her daughters studied their mother as she thought.

Amy ran a shaking hand over her face. "Yes," she whispered.

Katy's ears pricked up. "Really, which one?"

"All of them." Her voice lowered still so her words were difficult to hear.

"Mum, what are you saying? You know why Dad has been murdered?" Gemma asked.

"Possibly." Amy's gaze rose to meet Katy's.

"Would you rather tell me in private, without your daughters being present?"

"No. I'll need their support. One name stuck out for me."

"Who was that?"

"Bruce Crawford. He was a horrible man." She shuddered and paused to take a breath, then continued, "I don't know what happened, not truly, but something went on at his house years ago that had a truly devastating effect on Ellis."

Charlie whipped out her notebook and pen.

"Go on, please, anything you can tell us I feel sure will help capture this killer. Can you remember anything at all? Were you and Ellis married then?"

"Oh yes, we've been married since our teens. We met at school when we were thirteen. I know a lot of people say this, but Ellis truly was my soul mate. We had our children a few years after our life together began in earnest."

"How did he know Bruce?"

"I'll stand corrected if I'm wrong, but I think they met at the pub one night. There was a group of them. And yes, the other men you mentioned formed part of this group."

"Group or gang?" Katy needed to clarify.

"Not a gang, nothing as sinister as that, my Ellis would never have belonged to one of those. They were older by then, in their twenties when they started hanging around with each other. I suppose I'm partially to blame for that."

"You were? In what way?"

"Ellis was finding being a father of two young girls a little traumatic. He worked extremely long hours back then as a trainee manager, and to come home to these two, who always appeared to be bickering ten to twelve hours a day, took its toll on our relationship. I told him to get out and have some fun. I would've rather he did that than the alternative."

"Which would have been a separation or a divorce," Katy filled in the blanks.

"Yes. I knew deep down he loved me, he just needed the freedom to consider how much he loved, and appreciated, his family, if that makes sense? I wasn't one of these clingy wives. I trusted him implicitly, he'd never given me any reason not to."

"So what, these men would meet up regularly, is that right?"

"Yes, at the Dragon's Head around the corner from Bruce's home. Now and then they would have a drinking session at his house. Ellis said he didn't really like that much, he preferred it at the pub."

"Did he give a hint as to why?"

"Not really. Maybe he felt that it put too much pressure on Bruce's wife. If they chose to go there, she was expected to feed the men."

"I see. Go on." Katy sensed the woman was hesitating slightly and that what she was about to reveal could blow the case wide open. "Before you do, we've spoken to Adele Peters, the former wife of Dale. She intimated that something happened while the men were all together one night and their friendship appeared to end overnight. Is that your recollection of what went on?"

Amy licked her lips, and her head bounced in a nod. "Yes. I'm trying to recall the day it happened."

Katy tilted her head. "It? As in, the men falling out, or are you telling me you know what the falling out was about?"

"Please, give me time to work through this."

"Work through it? Mrs Bird, if you know what went on back then you need to tell us. It could prove significant to our investigation."

"Don't force the issue, I'm trying to get my mind around things."

Katy had a suspicion that the woman was going to come up with a cock-and-bull story that could have them jumping through hoops for days. *What are these men guilty of? And why is she willing to keep that secret from me?* "Would you rather take this down the station?" Katy snapped, she couldn't help it.

"Fuck off," Gemma said, leaping out of her seat again.

Her mother tugged on her arm, forcing her back down. "Don't do this. The inspector has a right to ask these questions. It's about time the truth came out."

"And what would that truth be, Amy? I can't tell you how important it is for you to divulge what you know in order for us to catch this killer."

"Do you seriously believe this has something to do with why my husband was killed?"

Katy shrugged. "Unless you tell us what you know, we have no way of knowing if that's true or not."

Amy dipped her head and placed her hands on her temples. "I should have said something years ago. I told Ellis to go to the police, but he refused."

"Mum, what are you saying? That Dad broke the law? How? You have to tell the police everything. What if the killer comes after you next?"

"Samantha, don't say that," Gemma shrieked.

"What? It could be true. How the fuck do we know unless she tells us? Jesus, I don't want to listen to this but, Mum, you have to tell the police. If you don't, you'll be putting all of us at risk. Are you willing to take a gamble on that?"

"Okay, maybe Sam has got a point, Mum. I hadn't thought of it that way. I don't want my husband or kids ending up in a mortuary...like Dad. Tell them what you know or..."

"Or what?" Amy stared at Gemma, worry lines etched into her forehead. "Are you threatening me, child?"

Gemma shrugged. "Make of it what you will. All I'll be doing is trying to protect my family."

"Ha...what do you think your father and I have been doing all these years?"

"Jesus, what are you saying? How big is this fucking secret you've been keeping from us for fuck's sake?" Gemma shouted.

"Stop swearing at me. Go, leave if you want. I don't want you here if you're going to speak to me like this."

Gemma reclined against the chair and folded her arms. She glowered at her mother and stated defiantly, "Tough. I ain't going anywhere until I hear you tell the truth."

"Please, can we all calm down? I appreciate your tempers are frayed at present, but arguing amongst yourselves isn't helping matters," Katy said, adrenaline speeding through her veins faster than any tsunami would likely carry it.

"She's right," Samantha said. "Mum, what's the point in keeping this secret any longer? If it's costing lives, you need to spit out what you know."

"I will. Stop bullying me, the pair of you."

"Your daughters are right. The sooner you tell us, the more likely we are to catch the person responsible. If we can do that, then there will be no need for you guys to live on your nerves, wondering if you'll be next." Katy felt Charlie's gaze on her. Yes, her statement had been over the top, but if it had the desired effect, and Amy finally revealed the secret she and her now-dead husband had concealed for years, it would be worth it.

"All right, don't hassle me, let me tell the story without interruptions. It is a heinous tale that has blighted my life for decades."

"Jesus, Mum!" Gemma shook her head in disgust.

"Let her say her piece," Samantha warned her sister.

Charlie had her pen poised, ready for action.

"Amy, tell us in your own time. We promise not to interrupt, right, girls?" Katy asked.

The two daughters reluctantly nodded.

Amy inhaled and exhaled a number of times and circled her neck as if to relieve the tension knotting her muscles. Katy was tempted to do the same. In the end, she sat perfectly still and studied Amy with interest.

"Where do I begin? Okay, the lads, all those you mentioned and another man, whose name escapes me at the moment, they used to meet up at the pub or Bruce's house—"

"You've told us that already, Mum. Get on with it," Gemma interrupted.

Amy's eyes doubled in size as she glared at her impatient daughter. "I warned you. Nope, I won't say any more."

Katy had heard enough. She rose to her feet, surprising everyone else in the room. "Right, Amy, get dressed, we'll continue this interview under caution down at the station."

"What? No, I can't do it. I won't do it!"

"Get dressed, or I mean it, I will throw the book at you for intentionally withholding vital evidence and perverting the course of justice."

"No, please. I had nothing to do with this. Wait, sit down, I'll tell you."

Katy pointed at the three women and wagged her finger. "This is a final warning. It's late, we all want to get to our beds, but we also want to hear the truth come out."

The three women seemed suitably reprimanded and each avoided eye contact with Katy.

"You were saying, Amy?"

"Okay, this one particular night, I remember Ellis coming home out of breath. His face was colourless. I asked him if he'd seen a ghost, and he shouted at me. I was flummoxed and hurt by his response. He was distraught for days. In the end, I couldn't take his mood swings any longer, he was starting to take his foul moods out on the girls. I was having none of that, they didn't deserve it. I noticed he wasn't going out, not seeing his friends. I tried to persuade him. He told me to stop nagging and to leave him alone. To my knowledge, I've never nagged him in over thirty years of marriage."

She reached out to hold each of her daughters' hands.

"Go on, Mum, you're doing well, don't stop now," Samantha encouraged her, smiling.

"I'm getting there, love." Amy sighed heavily and stared at the floor. "It was then he broke down and confessed what was bothering him. He said the night he came home distraught...he'd witnessed something horrendous. He later admitted that he was more involved than he first let on. I know that sounds confusing, but that's how it happened. The remorse brought the whole story out into the open. I was appalled, disgusted by the revelation. He feared I was going to walk out on him and take you girls with me. I thought about it long and hard but realised I wouldn't be able to bring you up on my own. We decided to work through the issue and never to discuss the matter again."

"Go on," Katy urged. She wished the woman would stop skirting around the issue and just reveal the truth.

"He said that night they had been involved in a sex game." She closed her eyes as if anticipating yet another outburst from her daughters. By the look of things, they were too shocked to say anything. "The game went wrong, and the woman ended up...being killed."

"Fucking hell," Gemma muttered.

She stared at her sister, and the tears began to fall for both of them.

Such a destructive revelation for any member of the family to hear, let alone his own daughters.

Katy's heart lay heavy in her chest. "Please, Amy, you need to reveal everything to us now, if only to protect your girls."

"How is informing the girls that their father was a sexual deviant going to save them?"

"The truth, Amy. We all need to hear it. Set yourself free from this suffocating secret. It's not yours to keep. The longer you suppress it, the more it's going to eat away at you."

"Twenty-four years I've pushed it down. It's eaten away at my soul. Destroyed my marriage."

Katy frowned. "In what way? You remained with Ellis once he told you."

"The sex. We never had sex after that night. It was my form of punishment. Such a shame; apart from that incident, he was an exceptional man and father to the girls."

"I hate him for what he put you through, Mum, *hate* him." Gemma spat the words out as she swiped at the tears resting on her cheeks.

"Don't say that, love. I should've taken the secret to my grave, that way your perception of him would still be intact. He loved you dearly."

"Jesus, how can you defend him? How could you put up with him, knowing that he'd killed a woman? Did you ever fear for your own life, or *ours*, Mum?"

"Don't think I haven't asked myself that same question thousands of times over the years. I knew I was taking a risk, but the alternative was so much harder to handle."

"Are you bloody listening to the shit that's tripping out of your mouth?" Gemma jumped to her feet and took a swipe at her mother's face.

Luckily, Samantha sensed what she was about to do and placed her arm in front of her mother to protect her. "Fuck off, Gem. Go home and calm down. Just reflect on your life and what your old man has done in the past. They're all the frigging same once they get you into bed, they think they own you outright and can do what they like."

"You fuck off. Leave Jimmy out of this, all that happened five years ago, we're happy now."

"What are you talking about? Happy, you don't know the meaning of the word. If you stripped off now, I bet you'd have dozens of bruises all over your scrawny body."

"Why, you!" Gemma pounced on her sister, managed to tug clumps of hair out of her head before Katy and Charlie could intervene and separate the warring siblings.

"Cut it out, the pair of you," Katy said. "Do you want me to call for backup, drag you all down the station? Because I will, in a bloody heartbeat. I need to ask your mother more questions. I'd rather do that in private if you're going to kick off like this. DC Simpkins, take Gemma and Samantha into another room while I continue to question Amy, will you?"

Charlie left her notebook on the sofa for Katy to use and marched the two sisters out of the room.

Amy sobbed and held her head in shame. "What have I done? I should have forced him to go to the police station. I'm so sorry. I've lived a life of hell knowing that I was covering for him and keeping that poor woman's death a secret."

Katy returned to the sofa and placed the notebook and pen on her lap. "I'm not denying you should have come forward sooner, Amy, however, there's little we can do about that now. You didn't tell me who this woman was. Was it someone they picked up off the street? A sex worker perhaps?"

"No, it was Bruce Crawford's wife."

The revelation rocked Katy. "What? Are you sure?"

"Absolutely. Why else would it cause a rift between the group of men?"

Katy scratched her head. "But you said this was a sex game gone wrong, can you elucidate on that?"

"Do I have to?"

"Yes. I need to know."

"I didn't know this until after…that night. Every time the men met up at Crawford's house, they either sexually abused the woman or tortured her in some way. Please, my girls have been through enough, they mustn't hear about this. They'll truly hate their father if any of this comes out."

"I can't guarantee that once the journalists get hold of the information, and they will, I assure you. That poor woman. I know this isn't what you want to hear right now and I appreciate you're grieving but I'm going to have to arrest you tonight."

Amy screamed. "No, you can't. I haven't done anything wrong."

Katy tutted. "You knowingly perverted the course of justice by not reporting a murder to the police and you also covered up for a murderer."

There was a tussle in the hallway. Katy jumped to her feet and wrenched open the door.

"What the hell is going on here?"

Poor Charlie was trying to fend off the two sisters who were determined to get to their mother.

"Is she all right? What have you done to her?" Gemma shouted in Katy's face.

"She's fine. Your mother will be coming back to the station with us."

"Why? She hasn't done anything wrong." Samantha tried to look beyond Katy into the lounge.

"I don't have to point out the gravity of the situation, you know what she's done wrong, your reactions were enough to convince me of that."

"You're arresting her?" Gemma screeched.

"That's right. I would advise you not to overact to the news and allow us to leave peacefully, otherwise, I'll be forced to arrest you both as well. What's it to be?"

The sisters stared at each other and, after a while, Gemma shrugged and Samantha nodded, accepting the situation was way beyond their control.

"Good. We'll be going now. You have my condolences about your father."

Gemma pointed behind Katy. "What about Mum? What's going to happen to her?"

"She'll be charged. I'm sorry, I don't have a choice at this stage. A woman was murdered, the family have a right to justice, and your mother should have had the courage to speak up earlier."

"We understand," Samantha told her.

"Go home. I'll ring you tomorrow, once I've spoken to your mother."

The girls, having now calmed down, passed Katy and went back into the lounge.

"Jesus, it's hard to contemplate what hell that woman has been living through all these years," Charlie leaned in to whisper.

"True, but it doesn't alter the fact that she should have spoken up sooner, Charlie. Two wrongs don't make a right, especially where murder is concerned."

"I hear you. So, who do you think is killing off these men?"

"Who do you think?" Katy had her suspicions, however, she wanted to hear Charlie's take on it.

"Are all the men dead? Could it be someone else was there that night and he's killed the others? Maybe someone threatened to expose them all."

"While it's a good theory, I'm inclined to believe I've been right all along."

"No! You still think it's Nadia?"

"Yep. Let's get Amy back to the station. She can spend the night in the cell, we'll question her tomorrow."

"What about Nadia?"

"I need to have a word with the chief first thing in the morning. If he backs up my theory then we'll bring her in for a taped interview."

"What a mess."

"I couldn't agree more. Let's get a wriggle on." She glanced at her watch. It was ten minutes after midnight, which depressed her. Another night of not tucking her child up in bed.

As if reading her mind, Charlie rubbed her arm. "There will be other nights."

"Will there? It's been a hell of a week thus far. Come on, there's no point in me being maudlin about this."

They left the house, accompanied by Amy Bird, and returned to the station. The desk sergeant said he wanted a word with Katy once she was free. Thinking that Amy wasn't about to kick up a fuss, Katy let Charlie deal with booking her in with the custody sergeant.

"All right, Ray, let me have it."

"It's about the car, ma'am."

Katy's interest piqued, swiping her weariness aside. "What about it?"

"We found it abandoned on a trading estate."

"Bugger. Get it picked up and sent to SOCO. Let's get the damn thing checked over, see what shows up."

"Already actioned, I figured you'd want that."

"Great stuff, thanks, Ray." Katy trudged upstairs to her office, debating on the journey whether she should call Roberts or not. She decided against the idea in the end.

Charlie joined her ten minutes later.

"Coffee?" Katy asked.

"I'd love one." Charlie flopped into her chair and placed her head in her hands.

Katy deposited the coffee on Charlie's desk. "You look cream-crackered, love. We'll have this and call it a day."

"We can't. The killer is still out there."

"Ah, but they've dumped the car. Ray on the front desk has just informed me. There's little we can do around here tonight."

"If you're sure. My brain is still whirling, it's just my body that's tired."

"I'm sure. It even crossed my mind to give the chief a call, but I dismissed that idea pretty swiftly."

"Maybe speaking to him in the morning will have cleared any possible doubts away."

"Doubts? I'm not sure I have any, Charlie, do you?"

Charlie blew at the steam escaping her cup and then took a sip. "I know you've said all along that you believe Nadia is the guilty party, but I'm not so sure."

"Why?"

"I just don't feel it's right. I can't tell you more than that."

"Fair enough. What we need to find out is the identity of the final member of the group."

"That's true. Either he's the guilty party or he might be able to point us in the right direction. But how are we going to locate him?"

"That's what's bugging me. I should've taken some photos of the people attending Crawford's funeral. Shame I didn't, we might have been able to save the other men's lives."

"Okay, we shouldn't blame ourselves, and there's a way around that."

Katy frowned and jabbed a finger at Charlie. "Nadia would know, after all, she was the one who sent out the invites for her father's funeral. Saying that, if she's the killer, she's hardly likely to give us the information, is she?"

"Catch-twenty-two situation. What if she's not the killer? If she can tell us the man's name, maybe we'll be able to save him before the killer strikes again."

"But you said yourself a few seconds ago that this man could be the one killing the others off."

"So I did. Bloody complicated working blind, with no clues or evidence to lead us, isn't it?"

Katy nodded. "Welcome to policing á la twenty-twenty where the criminals are getting smarter, some of them at least. We also need to fathom out why it's taken twenty-four years for the killer to make their move. Why all these years?"

"I haven't been able to get my head around that one yet, either. Something must have triggered them off to take this destructive route."

12

*K*aty arrived back at the station at eight-thirty the following morning, worn out but buzzing about what lay ahead of her that day. She chanced her luck and called in at Roberts' office before she stepped foot into the incident room. He was already at his desk.

"I'll check to see if he's accepting visitors this early, Inspector," Trisha said, surprised to see her.

"Tell him it's important, Trisha."

She disappeared into Roberts' office and closed the door. She emerged from the room a few seconds later and smiled at Katy. "Come through, Inspector. Can I get you both a cup of coffee?"

"That'd be lovely, thanks, Trisha," Sean replied. "Sit down, Katy. Is something troubling you?"

"One or two things I need to run past you regarding the investigation, sir," Katy said. She sat down opposite him, her leg muscles objecting during the movement.

Trisha entered with the drinks. She placed the tray on the desk, distributed the cups and saucers then left the room.

"Go on," Roberts said.

Katy ran through how the previous evening had panned out, the fact they were now investigating yet another murder, plus she let him know about the revelation Amy had given her.

"Bloody hell. Well, she'll go down for perverting the course of justice, won't she?"

"No doubt about it, sir. While I feel sorry for her, there's no way we can sit back and ignore what she and those men did all those years ago."

"I agree. So, are you any nearer to knowing who the killer is?"

"Charlie and I have discussed it at length and came to the conclusion that there are two possibilities."

"Which are?"

"My prime suspect throughout, Nadia Crawford, or we have to consider the possibility that the only man of the group in question who hasn't been murdered yet is the one responsible."

"And that person is?"

"Your guess is as good as mine on that one."

"What about the wife, Amy, is it?"

"Yeah, she couldn't tell me the bloke's name either. The only way I'm going to find out is by interviewing Nadia, but then, if she's the killer and is on a mission, is she likely to reveal his name if she has a score to settle?"

"Shitting hell. That is a terrible sodding dilemma for you to sort out."

"Which is why I'm laying it at your door."

Sean tipped his head back and laughed. "Right, so if you make the wrong call the onus lands on my desk, right?"

Katy grinned and then lifted her cup to take a sip of the richly roasted Colombian coffee she wished she was privy to more often than the vending machine shit she was forced to put up with. "I'm all ears."

"I'm sure you'll make the right decision come the end, Inspector."

She replaced her cup on its saucer. "Is that it? That's the only pearl of wisdom forthcoming from your direction?"

"Yes. I believe in you. I don't know how many more times I have to drum that into you, Katy Foster. Do what you deem necessary, and

I'll back you all the way." He leaned forward to retrieve his cup and winced.

"Are you okay or just seeking my sympathy?"

He pulled a face at her. "Had that been your former partner sitting there saying that, I would have expected to hear that. You've let me down, Katy."

She laughed. "Maybe she's still around poking me with a stick sometimes."

He rolled his eyes. "Now that wouldn't surprise me one iota. So, your next step is going to be what?"

"Well, we have Amy Bird in custody, but I'm inclined to let her stew in a cell for a few more hours. In the meantime, I think we need to pull Nadia in for an interview. I guess the reason I'm here is to ask your permission to do that."

Sean Roberts shook his head, his face darkening. "Bollocks, you do not want my advice, Katy. Do the right thing and bring her in, if that's what you think is needed. All I would advise is being cautious with her. Take a step back and assess all the evidence you've managed to gather so far, ask yourself if she's really capable of killing all these men and why."

"Okay. As long as you don't come down heavy on me if things go tits up."

"I won't."

Katy finished her coffee and left the room. She collected Charlie, who was just removing her jacket and placing it on the back of the chair, and they left the station.

They stopped off at Nadia's house first, just in case she was on a day off. Receiving no answer from the address, they made their way over to the hospital. It wasn't an ideal situation in Katy's mind, to show up at the woman's place of work, but what was the alternative?

Nadia was dealing with a male patient when they stepped foot on the ward.

She smiled and walked towards them carrying a bedpan. "Let me get rid of this and I'll be with you. I'm presuming you're here to see me."

"We are. Take your time," Katy replied, keeping things light, not wishing to alarm the woman in case she decided to bolt. She didn't have the strength in her legs to run after her if the notion emerged.

Nadia returned a few minutes later. "How can I help? Do you have news about my father's death?"

"In a way, yes. We're going to have to ask you to come with us to the station for an interview."

Nadia took a step back and threw a hand against her chest. "Me? Why?"

"Certain things have come to light during our investigation, and we'd like to know what your perception of them is."

"But I can't leave here. I'm working, and we're short-staffed as it is."

"It's okay. I'll have a word with your superior for you. Where am I likely to find her?"

"In the office around the corner."

"I'll be right back." She threw Charlie a look, telling her to keep a close eye on Nadia. Charlie nodded her understanding.

Katy knocked on the office door and spoke to a plump lady in a uniform. She flashed her ID and introduced herself. "Sorry to interrupt. I know you're short-staffed, but would it be okay if we borrowed Nadia for a few hours?"

"That's fine. We're actually fully staffed today, for a change."

"Ah, okay. Thanks for your assistance. We'll get her back soon." *Why had Nadia said they were short-staffed?*

The car was filled with a mixture of tension and silence on the return trip to the station. Katy had a word with the desk sergeant, asked him to try to locate a duty solicitor to oversee the interview, putting every precaution in place to cover Katy's back should her plan backfire.

The solicitor arrived fifteen minutes later. The four of them got acquainted in Interview Room One. Charlie started the tape and said the usual verbiage to get the proceedings underway.

"Thank you for agreeing to join us today, Nadia. We're hoping this interview won't take long so you'll be able to return to work shortly."

"Anything to help capture my father's killer, Inspector. I have to ask, is this usually how things are done? You dragging a member of the deceased's family in for questioning?"

"Sometimes it's necessary to get to the nitty-gritty of a story."

"I see. I have nothing to hide, so please, can we just get on with it?"

"Very well. First of all, I have a list of names I'd like you to look over." She pulled a sheet of paper from the file in front of her and slid it across the desk.

"Okay, what about them?"

"Perhaps you wouldn't mind telling me who these men are and how you know them?"

"They're all friends of my late father. I can't say I know them much. Although I met most of them recently when they attended my father's funeral. You were there, I believe."

"We were. I see. And when was the last time you saw any of these men?"

"Not since the funeral. Why? I don't understand why you're asking me this."

Her gaze held Nadia's as she said, "This week, all these men have lost their lives."

Nadia slammed back in her seat. "What? This can't be right. How?"

"Ah, that's where we're hoping you come in."

"I don't understand…no, you don't think I had anything to do with their deaths, do you?" Nadia sat forward. Her head swivelled between Katy and the solicitor. "She can't put me in the frame, can she?"

The solicitor shrugged, dipped her head and continued to take notes.

"We'll be asking you to verify where you were on certain dates. Of course, we'll need to confirm your alibis, especially as some other interesting news has materialised overnight."

"Are you going to tell me what that is?"

"Not yet." Katy then ran through the approximate times of death and asked Nadia where she was on each occasion.

"Most of those murders took place during my shifts at work. I have a rota to back me up on that, too. I swear, I had nothing to do with these deaths. I'm devastated that you should be trying to put me in the frame for these murders, especially after losing my father recently. Are you determined to push me over the edge, is that it?"

"Not at all. Talking of which, have you had any form of psychiatric evaluation done in the past?"

"I think you must be the crazy one for suggesting such a thing. No, I haven't. Do you seriously think I would be a nurse if I had mental issues?"

"It's been known in the past. Don't tell me you haven't heard of the Beverley Allitt case. She was a nurse on the prowl, wasn't she?"

"She may well have been, but you're forgetting one thing, Inspector." Katy tilted her head. "She killed the patients in her care."

"Fair enough. What I was referring to was the fact that she had a mental instability and yet she fooled those around her, her work colleagues and her superiors, in order to murder those poor children."

Nadia shook her head slowly, her gaze dropping to the table. "You're wrong." A tear dripped and spread across the Formica surface.

"Am I? What really happened with your father the night of his death?"

"I found him like that. He was barely conscious. I did all I could to try to save him, that's why I was covered in his blood, no other reason, I swear that's the truth. You're letting the killer get away, questioning me when they're still on the loose out there. Why aren't you listening to me? I'm *innocent*."

"Either you or your sister, I can't remember which of you, told me that your mother was dead. How did she die?"

"I don't remember," she muttered, her head still low.

"You must know. I remember a lot of insignificant things which happened in my life as a four-year-old. Are you telling me you're unable to recollect a significant detail such as how your mother died?"

"I can't. Father refused to talk about it. If you don't believe me, ask Penny, she'll tell you. Penny, yes, ring her, she'll verify what I've told you, I'm sure she will."

"Don't worry, we'll be contacting your sister soon enough."

Nadia glanced up. "Good. Maybe you'll believe her, if you're not prepared to believe what I'm telling you."

"What sort of upbringing did you have with your father?"

"Why?"

"I need to get some sort of background knowledge of your relationship. If I recall rightly, your sister had a fraught one with him, and she left home at the age of sixteen, and yet you remained in the house, why?"

"I had nowhere else to go."

"It didn't stop your sister from leaving."

"She's a stronger character than me."

"Why do you perceive yourself as being a weak character, Nadia?"

"I just am."

"Why? What happened twenty-four years ago?"

She shook her head, and another couple of tears dripped onto the table. "I can't...don't force me."

Katy faced Charlie and raised an eyebrow. She turned back to Nadia and said quietly, "What happened?"

"I can't...remember."

Katy slammed a fist onto the table, scaring everyone, including herself. "Tell me. I know you're keeping something from us."

"I'm not...I don't want to revisit...that time."

"Your father has abused you throughout your life, hasn't he?"

She nodded. "Yes. I had to do what he said, if I didn't..."

"What? What would he have done to you, Nadia?"

She sighed, and her head collapsed onto her arms. "I don't want to...please stop this...I've done nothing wrong. I'm being punished for his mistake. Please, don't do this."

"*His* mistake? Which was what?"

Nadia sobbed and ignored any further questions Katy put to her for the next five minutes. In the end, the solicitor called a halt to the interview.

"She needs a break. You're browbeating her. What good will that do, Inspector?"

"I need answers. Four men are residing in the mortuary fridge because of her. I need to find out why."

Nadia sat up and glared at Katy. Suddenly, she stood, tipped her chair back and flew at Katy, striking her in the face with her fist and clawing at her neck. Charlie raced around the desk and grappled with Nadia to restrain her. She slapped the cuffs on and righted the woman's seat then thrust Nadia in it.

"Sit down and don't move. Are you all right, boss?"

Katy took a tissue from her pocket and dabbed at her neck. "I'm fine. That attack was uncalled for, Miss Crawford. All you've succeeded in doing is proving that you have a violent nature and are capable of going on the attack when pushed into a corner."

"I'm sorry," she mumbled.

"Words are cheap. This interview will continue, I have no intention of drawing it to a conclusion, not yet."

"Okay by me," the female solicitor agreed, glancing sideways and giving her client a judgemental glare.

"No, I can't take any more. I'm sorry for lashing out, but you pushed me. You're not listening to me. I'm confused, that's why I went on the attack. No other reason, you have to believe me," Nadia said for what seemed to be the tenth time that morning.

"It's my job to get to the truth during an investigation, Nadia. Now, tell me what happened twenty-four years ago. For your information, I'm already aware. I need to hear it from you, though."

Her eyes widened, and she clenched her cuffed hands together. "You know?"

"Yes. We've only just found out. I want to hear your recollection of events."

"Okay. I'll tell you what I know. The other night, after my father died, I had a nightmare, it's the only recollection I have of what happened that night. I can't tell you how accurate the memory is. This is the truth. I fear all I'm guilty of is blocking the image from my mind. It was horrendous, not something a child of four should have seen."

"Go on."

"That night…" She stared at the names on the list to the side of her.

"These men, all of them, took a turn in raping my mother. Can you imagine the trauma I must have gone through as a child seeing that?"

"I can't, it must have been hideous. Did it happen the once or numerous times?"

"A number of times to my knowledge, always in the cellar. They bound her to a table and gagged her to prevent her from screaming. The men laughed and were eager to take it in turns. This particular night, their sex game went too far. One of them strangled her. They all panicked. I ran back to my bedroom. I heard a noise outside and raced to the window. They carried my mother's body in a rug, at least, I'm presuming it was her. Someone noticed the curtain move. My father ran up the stairs to our room. I had to pretend to be asleep. I think he was aware of what I saw that night and punished me for the rest of my life. With my mother out of the way, he got his kicks from raping me."

"Is that why you killed him?" Katy asked softly.

"I didn't kill him, as much as I've wanted to over the years, I *didn't do it.*"

And at that point in the investigation, Katy believed the young woman sitting opposite her. She had nothing to back up her claims to believe Nadia was guilty.

"How far did the abuse go, for you, I mean?"

Nadia gulped. "It was constant, from the moment my mother…died to well into my teens."

"Not lately?"

"No. I think I was around nineteen when he finally stopped coming into my room at night."

"Why didn't you leave with your sister?"

"Please don't ask me that, I've been asking myself the same thing for years. Penny has a courage that knows no bounds. She knew what he was doing was wrong from the outset." She jabbed at her temple with her shaking hand. "I don't know, but maybe seeing my mother get killed that night…I don't know what I want to say because in my head none of this makes sense."

"You believe you owed it to your father to be a stand-in wife, is that what you're suggesting?" Katy asked quietly, trying to get around how a four-year-old growing into her teens could possibly justify any form of abuse. She had no concept of what ran through kids' minds who found themselves in such dire situations, having never had to deal with such atrocities herself.

"I don't know. It's hard to call it how it is, Inspector. He was my father. Rather than feel his wrath, I did things that may seem unnatural to others. Thinking back now, it sickens me to think of…it repulses me, but he was my father, and I loved him in spite of all his faults."

"There's no greater love than that between a father and his daughter, I appreciate that. I love my father with a passion, but he's never abused me. Did you try to seek help at all?"

She inhaled a deep shuddering breath that inflated her chest. "I thought about it once but I couldn't go through with it."

"Do you know why?"

"Purely selfish reasons. I knew if my father was put in prison I would have been taken into care. No one could convince me the same thing wouldn't have gone on in someone else's home."

"Believe me, the care system isn't like that. I've maybe heard of a smattering of cases over the years, but they have all been dealt with promptly."

"You see? How could I take the risk? Better the devil you know, eh?"

"Did you ever raise the subject of your mother's death with him? Was he aware in later life of what you saw that night?"

"No. Like I told you earlier, what happened to my mother appeared to have been stored away in the deep recesses of my mind until the other night when the nightmare resurfaced."

"And that was *after* his death, right?"

"Yes, after his death."

"Okay, if I'm to believe what you're telling me to be the truth, why do you think these men have been killed, and more importantly, who do you think might be killing them?"

"Gosh, how could I possibly know that? I'm as shocked and surprised to learn about the other deaths today. The only one I knew about was Dale Peters because you've already questioned me and asked me for an alibi relating to his murder, am I right?"

"Correct. It would really help if you told us the other man's name? Was he at the funeral?"

"I'm guessing he was, there were four pallbearers. I have his name and contact details at home in my father's address book, that's how I was able to get in touch with the men, to ask them to attend."

"We'll need that. Are you sure you can't think of his name at least?"

She picked up the list and narrowed her eyes to study it as she thought. "Keith, that's who is missing. I can't for the life of me think of his surname, though. That's the best I can do, I'm sorry."

"It's okay. I think we're done here anyway."

"Does that mean I can go?"

"Yes."

"You no longer suspect me?"

"I think I'm willing to draw a line under that for now, on one proviso."

"I'm listening."

"That you have a psych evaluation."

"Of course, anything, anything at all. I'm so sorry for attacking you. I had to make you see sense, that I am an innocent victim in all of this."

Katy smiled at her. "I believe you. I'll survive a few surface bruises and scratches. I'm more concerned about how you're going to cope going forward."

"Despite my father's death, I've been coping all right. I've thrown myself into work, which has helped and prevented me from sitting at home dwelling on his death and what happened to my mother all those years ago."

"I can imagine. I'll get someone to drop you back home. If you'll give them the information about the fifth man, his name and address if you have it."

"I do have it, I just can't remember it off the top of my head. Thank you for believing in me. I know you don't have to, and I think other officers would feel differently to how you do."

"Okay, then you're free to go. You have my number. If you think of anything else relevant to the investigation or what happened to your mother, please let me know."

"I will. I promise you."

Charlie ended the taping session, and everyone rose from their seats and left the room.

Katy thanked the solicitor for attending and then spoke to the desk sergeant. "Ray, have you got a car available to run Miss Crawford home?"

"I can sort that out for you immediately, ma'am, leave it with me."

"Thanks."

Katy went back to Charlie and Nadia. "If you take a seat, a uniformed officer will give you a lift home ASAP. Just a reminder, give them the address for Keith before they leave, if you would."

"I will. Thank you for understanding, Inspector. I'll wait to hear from you regarding the other details you mentioned."

"I'll arrange for you to be evaluated shortly. Speak soon."

Nadia sat on the seat closest to the door, and Katy and Charlie walked upstairs to the incident room.

Charlie flopped into her chair. "What do you think? Before you answer that—"

"No, it's not what I think that matters, you tell me what you think."

"I was just going to say, I understand you asking her to take a psych eval, but isn't there an illness where someone does something unknowingly? Like they switch off and allow another personality to take over?"

"Maybe. There's a condition called Split Personality Disorder or whatever it's known as nowadays, but I'm not sure how far the person would go. I need to do some research. You go home, I'll work through and get things organised."

"No way. I'm here for the duration. Will you be able to contact a shrink at this time of night? Oops...it's now morning."

Katy spun around and glanced at the clock. It was one-thirty. "Shit,

I didn't realise that was the time. Looking on the bright side, not long to go before our shift is supposed to start, right?"

They both laughed.

"There is that. Shall I get us a coffee? We're going to need one to help us stay awake," Charlie proposed.

"Good idea. I'll boot up your computer, and we can bounce some ideas around."

---

13

*B*y the time the rest of the team had arrived, Katy felt she knew every clinical term possible for what they were conceivably dealing with.

Charlie had nipped out for a bacon roll each at around seven when they knew the café would be open. Which gave them the sustenance needed to continue their working day.

Katy filled the team in on what had come up over the past few days: the murder of Ellis Bird, the fact his wife was sitting in a cell still —she'd get around to interviewing her within the next couple of hours. The interview with Nadia had hampered things there the day before. There was no getting away from the fact that Amy Bird knowingly covered up the murder of Nadia's mother twenty-four years previously. Plus, now they had the final man's name—there was work to do there as well.

"I think we need to put this man under surveillance. My thinking is that either he's the murderer, knocking off all his friends, or he'll turn out to be the final victim."

"Should we haul his arse in for his part in Nadia's mother's murder?" Graham asked the obvious question.

"That's our ultimate dilemma. If we do that and he's out of the scene, how are we going to catch the murderer, if he's not the guilty party? Am I talking nonsense? My brain's gone to mush."

"No, I get where you're coming from," Charlie backed Katy up.

"Good. So, who's up for sitting in their car for God knows how long?"

Graham tutted. "Okay, I'll do it. Patrick, are you up for it?"

"As long as I don't have to listen to bloody U2 all day long like the last time I paired up with you."

"All right, guys, cut it out. I need you to take up your post now. Ring me if anything happens. We have a few loose ends to sort out in your absence."

The two men leapt to their feet and exited the incident room.

Karen coughed and cleared her throat. "All right if I chip in with something in light of what you told us, boss?"

"Go ahead, Karen, feel free."

"What about the sister, Penny?"

Katy tilted her head. "What's on your mind?"

"Could she be the killer? She has the motive to kill her father because of the abuse. Not sure about the other men, though."

"Hmm…it's a thought. Do some digging for me. Let's see if she's still up in Scotland for a start. I forgot to ask Nadia if her sister was aware of how her mother died. Maybe she kept the secret from her sibling."

"That's a definite possibility if Nadia is telling us that she's kept it hidden for all these years."

Katy went over to the whiteboard and added all the facts they'd gathered overnight to the other information noted down. "I'm going to visit the chief, keep him up to date."

"Want me to ring the psychiatrist on call?" Charlie offered.

"Yes, if you would, Charlie. Tell them that the matter is an urgent one and we need that psych report ASAP."

"I will."

"I'll be back in a tick." Katy set off and walked the length of the corridor to the DCI's office.

Trisha smiled. "Back again so soon, Inspector?"

"I might as well set up a desk in his office, eh?"

"I'm sure that would go down well with his nibs."

"Hey, at least I'll have fancy coffee on tap." Katy winked as Trisha left her desk and knocked on the chief's door.

"DI Foster to see you if you have a spare moment, sir."

"Send her in," Roberts replied.

Trisha stepped back and smiled. "Can I get you a coffee?"

"That would be lovely, thanks, Trisha."

Katy entered the office.

Sean was eyeing her suspiciously. "Inspector, to what do I owe the pleasure?"

"Thought I'd drop by to bring you up to speed on the developments we encountered overnight, sir."

"Okay, first of all, sorry, take a seat, I have some news for you."

"Sounds ominous."

"I know it's taken a while to surface, and I bet you thought I'd forgotten about it, but I hadn't."

"Are you going to give me a hint about what you're referring to, sir?"

"The incident with the gun leaving the evidence room in your previous case. DC Wainwright turned out to be the culprit. He admitted the charge against him plus asked several others to be taken into consideration. Apparently, some of the gang's drugs and arms were seized, and he handed them back to the gang after they blackmailed him and threatened to kidnap his teenage daughter and hand her over to a human trafficking ring."

"Fuck. So he did it under duress. Will the powers that be go lightly on him in that case?"

"They'd better. We're hearing more and more about this type of thing happening to our members, it's a wonder people still want to sign up to join the police."

"It's a scary thought. AJ and I discussed this not long ago with regard to me changing my name. That's settled, I'll keep to Foster at work. The last thing I want to do is put AJ and Georgie in jeopardy."

Trisha walked in with two cups of coffee and distributed them.

"Thank you, Trisha. I'm sure this is the only reason DI Foster insists on making these frequent visits to my office."

Katy pulled a mock-offended face. "How dare you insinuate that, sir? Is that the thanks I get for pulling an all-nighter?"

"Okay, maybe I've misjudged you. What do you think, Trisha?"

"I'm keeping out of it, sir, if you don't mind. I enjoy working here." Trisha left them to it.

"Anyway, he'll plead his case with the IPCC, probably get a rap on the knuckles, nothing more now that the gang has been wiped out and is no longer in existence."

Katy sipped her smoothly roasted coffee and then nodded. "There's bound to be another gang take their place soon enough, there always is. Charlie's organising a psych evaluation for Nadia—there's still a possibility she's our suspect. It might be a case of Dissociative Identity Disorder as they refer to it these days. I'm an expert on the topic now, or I should be after the hours Charlie and I have put in researching the damn subject."

"Is there such a thing? You're telling me you think she's killed these men without realising that she's done it?"

"I know it sounds far-fetched, I hope I'm wrong, but the mind is a complex organ. If, as she stated, she's suppressed the images of her mother's death until recently, who knows what's going on in her head?"

"But she's a nurse, should she still be performing her duties?"

Katy sighed and puffed out her cheeks. "That's the sixty-four-million-pound question. All this is supposition on my part, we don't have any evidence at this point to back up either my claims, or her guilt or innocence."

"It's a puzzle we need to unravel soon."

"There's another thing. The car the witness spotted leaving the Bird murder scene has also been found, dumped on a trading estate."

"Well, that's good news. I take it Forensics have it now."

"Yep, first thing I asked when it was found. The desk sergeant had already actioned the request."

"Glad to hear the team are on the ball. What are your plans for the wife of the latest victim? That's a tough call because you've had a grieving woman locked up in a cell for two nights now."

"I'm aware of that. I don't know whether to feel guilty or take pride in hauling her in."

"Odd conclusion, I must say. She needs to be charged and released, Katy."

"I know. That's my next task, well, after I get a statement of events from her first."

"You'd better get a move on then, time's a wasting, as they say."

"Can't I finish my coffee first, after slaving all night?"

"All right. There's no need to keep playing the martyr."

Katy chuckled. "Worth a try." She downed the rest of her coffee and sprang out of her seat. "I could drop by with another update at around one, if that's all right with you, sir?"

"Get out, you, cheeky scoundrel."

Katy reached the door and flashed him a smile. "Shoot me for trying. What about if I get an intravenous line running along the corridor tapped into your coffee machine?"

"I'd snip it halfway down. Now go."

There was a lightness in her steps as she made her way back to the incident room. It felt good to have a bit of banter first thing to ease the stress running through her during an investigation.

"Any luck, Charlie?"

"Yep, managed to book an appointment with a Doctor Marlow for seven o'clock this evening. Do you want me to call Nadia and tell her when and where to attend?"

"If you would. Thanks. I'm just going to give AJ a call and then I'll go down and interview Amy Bird. Oh, by the way, we have an update on the missing gun from the evidence room. An officer has been named, and it's in the hands of the IPCC. He was coerced into doing the deed, shall we say."

"That's terrible, guv, are any of us truly safe?" Karen asked.

"It makes you wonder, Karen. Have you managed to find out anything about Penny Wallender?"

"I was a tad sneaky there. I rang her home number and pretended to be someone from the gas board. I told her there'd been a leak reported a few doors down and asked if she'd been present in the house all week and had she noticed any strange smells lately. She said she'd been at home all that time, mourning the loss of her father."

"Good thinking, Karen. Well, that appears to rule her out of the equation. I won't be long." She drifted into her office. The post had already been dealt with when it had arrived earlier, so she didn't have that mindless chore to deal with.

She called AJ on her mobile. He answered after a few rings. "Hello, sweetheart, just checking in on my favourite two people."

"Hey, you. We're fine, how are you holding up?"

"Ditto. I can't talk for long, I have someone I need to interview, she'll be well stewed by now. What are you guys up to today?"

"You're not missing out on much. Playschool this morning, and then I thought I'd take the little minx to the park for a picnic, if the weather stays fine."

"That'll be wonderful for her. You're such a thoughtful dad, AJ."

"Am not. It's what any father would do, given the chance, I'm sure."

"I doubt it. Do you have enough food in? Don't go giving her all carbs. Bung in some fresh fruit and raw veggies like celery and carrot sticks. Damn, what am I saying? You know all this."

"I do. I don't blame you for checking, though. Thanks for that. Are you tired?"

"No, not at the moment. I've just had a welcome Colombian coffee with the boss that'll keep me satisfied and functioning properly for a while."

"I bet it'll hit you around lunchtime. If you're in the area, drop by the park, we'll be there from around one, if I get my act together. I'll make up an extra serving for you and Charlie just in case. Georgie and I can always have it for lunch tomorrow if you're a no-show."

"We'll do our best. The park at the end of the street?"

"That's the one. I don't want you getting jealous, though. I've arranged to meet up with a few of the other mothers down there."

"No fear of that, love. I haven't got time to get jealous. Anyway, I trust you implicitly."

"The same here."

"I have to shoot off now, AJ. I love you, don't ever forget that."

"I won't. I love you, too, Katy. I think you're a wonderful mother and DI to boot."

"Why thank you, kind sir." She ended the call and dabbed her eyes with a tissue. "Silly woman, turning to mush like that."

Charlie appeared in the doorway. "Oh God, is everything all right?"

"Yep, just hubby and I getting all sentimental with each other."

"You're entitled to do that after working all night. Is he okay about you not going home last night?"

"Yeah, he was fine. He understands it only happens now and then. Did you manage to contact Nadia?"

"Yeah, she's agreed to the appointment."

"Great stuff. I forgot to ask you to mention to the doctor why we needed the appointment."

"All in hand. I filled him in. Can I speak freely?"

"Of course, always, you know that, Charlie. Come in, take a seat."

Charlie closed the door behind her and sat.

"What's on your mind?"

"It's a bit of an out-of-the-box idea, and I swear I haven't been speaking to Mum about any of this, just in case you aim that one at me."

"Go on, I trust you."

"You know what we're up against, a missing body of the victim from twenty-four years ago...well, I wondered if it would be worth having a chat with—"

Katy held her hand up. "Stop right there, I know what you're going to say. You want me to get Carol involved, right?"

"Trust me, I'm in two minds whether to contact her myself, but surely, it would make sense, wouldn't it?"

Katy contemplated, for a good few minutes, her partner's suggestion of bringing the psychic in to help before she found the voice to answer her, "Okay, I think you have a point. Why not? Will you call her, or shall I?"

Charlie's teeth showed through her parting lips. "I think it would make her day if you rang her."

"Get me the damn number then. Do you think she'll do it over the phone? Or will she need to come here?"

"Not sure, ask her. I think you'll be pleasantly surprised with what she can do, and she'll be thrilled to know that you thought of her."

"Correction, I didn't think of her, *you* did. This is between you and me, right? If Roberts hears about this…he'll strike me off as being a loon and for taking after your mother."

"You reckon? I'll get my phone." Charlie nipped out of the office and returned within seconds. "Here you go. Want me to hang around while you make the call?"

"Go on then, I'll put it on speaker, in case I miss anything. Wish me luck." Katy punched in the number and waited for Carol to pick up.

"Hello. Who is this?" Carol asked suspiciously as Katy's phone would have come up with a 'number withheld' status.

"Carol, it's DI Katy Foster. I'm not sure if you'll remember me or not, we worked on the Noelle Holten case together."

"Of course, I remember you, dear. Lorne's sceptical partner."

"That's the one. Although in all fairness, by the end of that case I was a true believer in your abilities, if you recall correctly."

"Hmm…I suppose I remember the outcome differently to you. Anyway, this is a surprise. What can I do for you?"

"First of all, Charlie's here listening in, she was the one who suggested I should call you."

"Aww…hi, Charlie, long time no hear, love. How are you?"

"Sorry, Carol. I'll remedy that soon. We're in the middle of working a hectic case."

"I know all about it, dear. I've been sitting here twiddling my thumbs, waiting for you to get in touch to ask for my help."

"Oh my. Dare I ask what you know, Carol?" Katy jumped in.

"Well, first of all, I have four men sitting here with me. Want me to give you their names?"

"Why not?"

"All righty then. I've got Bruce, Dale, Robin and Ellis around me now, ladies. What do you want to ask them?"

"Where do you start?" Katy whispered to Charlie.

"At the beginning," Charlie responded, then chewed on her lip anxiously.

"Okay, Carol, perhaps the gents wouldn't mind telling us what went on that night twenty-four years ago."

"I'll ask. Oh dear, a few of them have bowed their heads in shame. All right, boys, let's have it." A few moments of silence passed before Carol spoke again. "Most of them are remorseful, with one exception, Bruce. He's telling me she deserved what she got."

"Why am I not surprised to hear that?" Katy replied. "Let's ignore him for a moment and concentrate on the others, Carol."

"As you want. Come on, guys, let's help the police officers out here. Tell me what happened." Another lull was followed by Carol gasping.

"Are you all right, Carol?"

"I'm fine. Oh my, that poor defenceless woman. You men should be ashamed of yourselves for putting her through that. And you, Bruce, you're a despicable piece of shit. I hope Hell welcomes you with open arms for treating your wife, and daughters, come to that, in such a horrendous way."

"What's going on, Carol?" Katy queried, eager to know.

"That night, like many others before, all the men raped Sonia Crawford. Things went too far. They tried something different to add to the thrill. Two of them tried strangling her and, well…their little game went too far and she died."

"Okay, that account matches up with what we already know, Carol. Thank them for their honesty." The words stuck in Katy's throat. Why should she thank a bloody murderer, least of all a dead one, communicating with her through a medium? It was beyond her but a necessity all the same, if they were going to find out where the body was buried. "I need to know what happened to her body once it left the house and was placed in the boot of the car."

Carol then asked the spirits who surrounded her the question. "Right, okay, they're telling me that Sonia is buried in a forest. Which one...? Shendon Forest, do you know it, Katy?"

Charlie picked up her phone and did the relevant search. She angled the phone in Katy's direction.

"Yep, I've got it. They need to give me more than that. How far in? Any markers to identify where?"

"Come on, guys, you can do better than that. Where exactly is she buried?"

The silence in between the questions was killing Katy. She gestured for the proceedings to go faster, and Charlie chuckled.

"Okay, I have a location for you. There's an opening trail that leads into the woods. Take the right fork and go twenty feet or so. On the right, there's a marker of sorts, at least there was back then, they're telling me. She's buried there, still wrapped in the rug."

"Thanks, Carol. Dare I ask if Sonia's spirit is there with you?"

"No. She wouldn't show up, not with this mob present. I'll leave it a while and try to contact her later. I'll call you if I succeed."

"You're a star, thanks, Carol. Speak soon."

"Katy, I'm glad you rang. I'm always here at your disposal, remember that."

"Thanks. Will do. I'd better go and get on the phone to organise a search of the forest."

"Good luck. Love to both of you. Don't be a stranger, Charlie."

"I won't. I've been working flat out, Carol. I'll make it up to you soon, I promise."

"I know you have. You're in my thoughts, ladies."

Katy ended the call and lifted her office phone. "Bring the team up to date, will you, Charlie? I won't be long."

Charlie rushed out of the room and closed the door behind her.

"Patti, sorry to trouble you. I have some news."

"Go on, surprise me."

Katy filled her in on what Carol had revealed and asked for assistance. "Can we get SOCO over there to check it out?"

"I can arrange that for you. I might even take a wander out that way myself if I can finish the next PM promptly. How exciting. Sorry, that sounded bad. I didn't mean it to come across that way. I meant after all this time, it'll be a relief to finally lay that woman to rest properly, not in a pauper's grave. And good on Carol for playing her part in all this as well."

"We'll see if what she told us turns out to be the truth or not. I wouldn't put it past these men to be winding us up even through their spirits."

"There is that. Let me get the ball rolling. See you out at the site later."

"Definitely. Thanks, Patti."

Katy sat back after ending the call and reflected on whether she was doing the right thing or not, taking the word of four spirits. She shook her head. It sounded unreasonable to consider, but at this point, she was willing to do just about anything to get a result. Maybe Sonia's spirit would show up soon and talk to Carol, possibly even reveal who the damn killer was.

She joined the rest of the team not long after. "Charlie, come on, we'll take a leisurely drive over there. I want to be there when they start digging. I hope it doesn't turn out to be a false alarm."

"I'm sure it won't. Have faith in Carol's abilities, she's never let Mum down in the past, has she?"

Katy cast her mind back and had to admit, she couldn't think of a time when Carol had failed them. "You're right, let's hope this isn't the first time."

14

The forest was a well-known walkers' paradise in the local area, but even on a bright August day there was an eeriness to it. The paths were well cared for. A sign told Katy that the upkeep was down to the National Trust. "Looks like SOCO are already here."

"Wonder how long it will take them to set up." Charlie peered through the dense area ahead.

"I shouldn't think it would be too long."

"Hello again, ladies, nice of you to join us." Patti startled them both by sneaking up behind them.

Katy spun around, her hand covering her chest. "Holy shit! Thanks, Patti, as if this place isn't creepy enough already."

"Sorry. Shall we?" Patti marched ahead, expecting them to join her.

"If I can slow my heart rate down to near normal, yes, we'll be right with you."

"Wuss!" Patti shouted over her right shoulder.

The SOCO technicians were organising themselves into a frenzy.

Patti needed to step in and call a halt to the proceedings before things got out of hand. "I appreciate how eager we all are to get started, but let's stick to protocol, guys. Less haste, more speed and all that. Got it?" She turned to face Katy and Charlie and dipped a hand into her bag. She withdrew a couple of protective suits and flung them in their direction. "You know the drill, even if this does turn out to be an extremely old crime scene."

Katy and Charlie quickly stepped into their suits and joined Patti a few feet away.

"This appears to be the right area according to the directions you gave me via you know who." Patti winked at Katy.

Katy raised her crossed fingers and held her breath as two technicians began to dig carefully, half a shovel depth at a time.

They were thirty minutes into the dig when one of the men hit something and alerted Patti.

"All right, John, nice and slowly, scrape back the earth around the object. Try not to disturb it too much."

Charlie clutched Katy's arm and then apologised.

"It's fine," Katy said. "I feel apprehensive as well. Let's hope this is the right spot."

The men scratched the soil away, placing it in a pile on a groundsheet for further analysis later. John beckoned Patti, who in turn gestured for Katy and Charlie to join her.

"What is it?" Katy asked. She stared at some form of material and then gasped as the realisation dawned on her. "Oh. My. God. Is that a rug?"

"Seems to me your assumption is spot on, Inspector. Guys, let's have some more hands over here now. Gently does it. I couldn't give a toss if we turn out to be here all day, let's try not to disturb too much with the shovels, use your hands if necessary."

Another two men joined in. Twenty minutes later, they had uncovered a rug that was frayed and fragmented. Patti tugged one long piece from the hole and laid it on the groundsheet. This was followed by numerous other six- to eight-inch squares. Katy peered into the hole left behind and shook her head.

"What's wrong?" Charlie asked, confused.

"It's just a rug. There should be bones in there, but there's nothing. Can you confirm what I'm seeing, Patti?"

"I think your postulation is accurate, Katy. Let's see what the men can find lower down. My prediction is that the rug was probably wrapped around the woman's body numerous times. As you say, there are no bones at present. Hopefully that status will change the deeper we dig."

A bad feeling swept through Katy. The more the men dug, the more her heart sank. "She's not here," she leaned over and whispered to Charlie.

"Hang tight. She must be. Where else would she be?"

Katy cocked an eyebrow at her partner. "Have you seen the size of London? Shit, they could have put her anywhere."

Charlie shook her head. "It doesn't make sense. Why would the men lead us to this location if she's not buried here? Furthermore, why would the men bury just the rug?"

Katy raised her arms and then slammed them against her thighs. "I don't frigging know." Then she gasped. "What if one of them returned to exhume the body?"

"What? Why would they do that?"

"I don't know. None of this investigation has made any sense so far. I suppose anything and everything is possible, isn't it?"

"Sadly, yes, that's true. Should we ring Carol, see if she has anything further to add now that we're here?"

"It's worth a shot."

Charlie took a few steps back and rang her friend. She returned with disappointment clouding her features. "She's as flummoxed as we are."

"Brilliant...not. Did she have any luck trying to make contact with the woman's spirit?"

"She's tried, but her powers are failing her at the moment. She's putting it down to exhaustion after summoning up the men earlier."

"Makes sense. I forgot how draining connecting with spirits can be for her. Maybe we'll give her a while and then call back, it wouldn't hurt to give her a nudge later."

"I'm sure she'll get in touch with us soon enough."

Patti joined them, her shoulders slumped in resignation. "My apologies, ladies, I think we're barking up the wrong tree here. Sorry for the inexcusable poor pun. Forensics will be able to tell if a body had been in the rug, so all is not lost."

"Are we, though? The rug is here even if her body isn't. We're thinking along the lines that maybe one of the men might have returned to dig up the body. Jesus, we need to go and see Keith."

Patti frowned and thrust her hands on her hips. "Who's he?"

"He's the surviving member of the group, the only one still alive. I have him under surveillance in case the murderer goes after him. Come on, Charlie, sod waiting around here for something that's not going to materialise."

They ripped off their suits, deposited them in the black bag and raced back to the car.

Once they were on the way, Katy asked Charlie to call Patrick and put it on speaker phone. "Patrick, it's me. Anything?"

"He's inside, boss. No sign of him going out, and no one has shown up from what we can tell."

"Good. We're on our way over there to see him. We've just located the burial site, except the body was nowhere to be seen. I'm banking on him telling us what he knows. We're thinking along the lines that one of the men may have possibly returned and dug the woman up, maybe to give her a proper burial. Ugh...pure speculation, who sodding knows if that's true or not?"

"Whoa! That's some wacky theory, boss, if you don't mind me saying? How long will you be?"

"Tell me about it. We're twenty-five minutes out according to the satnav."

"See you soon then. Any movement, we'll give you a bell."

"Do that." She nodded for Charlie to end the call.

*T*hey pulled up outside Keith Pittman's house. Situated in a quiet suburban road, it was semi-detached with a pretty front garden in full bloom with dahlias planted amidst dozens of rose trees of various colours and varieties.

Katy stopped off to talk to Patrick and Graham first. "We'll go in. Any problems...just be alert at all times."

"Are you sure you don't want either of us to go in there with you?"

"I think we'll be fine. I've got a few questions to ask, and then we'll take him down the station to book him on a murder charge." Katy joined her partner at the gate. "You ready for this? It could go one of two ways, you know that, don't you?"

Charlie withdrew her hand from her jacket pocket and waved the can of pepper spray. "I'm all prepared."

"Let's go." Katy rang the bell.

A man in his mid-fifties answered the door almost immediately. "Yes. Can I help?"

"I think you can, Mr Pittman." Katy flashed her ID in his face. "All right if we come in for a moment?"

"Not until you tell me what this intrusion is all about."

"Intrusion? Okay, we're investigating several murders in the area and—"

"And what? You think I have something to do with them? Are you crazy? I'm a law-abiding citizen, I would never..."

Katy smiled and inclined her head. "You were saying? Don't let me stop you. Why pause? Unless you know that's not the truth, sir. Are you going to let us in?"

He spun on his heel and stormed ahead of them, up the hallway and into the first room on the right, which turned out to be a through-lounge divided by an arch which led into a dining area.

"What do you want from me?" He paced the floor, close to the TV.

"Take a seat, sir. We'd like to ask you a few questions."

The three of them sat, and Charlie withdrew her notebook from her pocket and flipped it open.

He stared at Katy and said, "I know nothing."

"I haven't asked you anything yet. As I said, we're investigating several murders in the area which took place in the past week or so. I believe the victims are all people you know, sir."

"What? Who?"

"Bruce Crawford, Robin Hewitt, Dale Peters and Ellis Bird."

With each name she mentioned, his mouth gaped open wider, and the colour drained from his reasonably tanned face.

"No way...this can't be true."

"I'm afraid it is. Now, what we'd like to know is, who do you think killed them?"

"How should I fucking know? What is this? I haven't done anything wrong."

"Let's set the recent murders aside for a moment. How about you tell me why you and the four men I've just mentioned killed Sonia Crawford?"

His left hand covered his eyes, and he wailed, "It wasn't down to me. I wanted no part in it. *He* forced me to do it."

"Who did?"

"Bruce. He was a bully. If you didn't do as he said, he could cause trouble for you, if you see what I mean?"

"So rather than stand up to him, you went ahead and robbed that poor *defenceless* woman of her life."

"I'm sorry. I've regretted my actions all these years." He pointed to a shelf on the bookcase. "I take forty-odd tablets a day because of what happened back then. I've been in and out of hospitals, mental hospitals because I can't get rid of the images from that night."

"So, what you're telling us is you have a conscience, yes?"

"Yes. I suppose so."

"Not enough of one to want to turn yourself, and the others, in to the police, though, right?"

"I've tried numerous times. Plucked up the courage to go down the cop shop, only to back out at the last minute. Please, you have to believe me."

"Oh, I do. Unable to fight your conscience any longer, you thought you'd kill your so-called friends instead, is that it?"

He stared at her, his expression one of horrified confusion as her words sank in. He eventually jumped out of his seat and paced the room again. "No, you've got this all wrong. I would never..."

"What? Commit murder? That's a lie, and you know it, Mr Pittman."

"It was an accident all those years ago. We didn't mean to kill her, we were only having a laugh."

"You perceive raping and strangling a woman as a laugh, a game? How warped are you? All of you."

He paced and fell silent. After a while, he stopped and stared at them. "I didn't want any of this. It's so wrong for you to come here and challenge me about this after all these years."

"We found the burial site."

"What? That's impossible."

"It's not. We found it. The only trouble is, Sonia Crawford's body wasn't there. Now, why do you suppose that is, sir?"

"Shit! How the fuck should I know? She was there. We all saw her placed in the ground. We all did our bit to dig that hole deep enough so that she would never be discovered."

"If you were all involved, why kill off your associates?"

"I haven't, I'm telling you. You have to believe me, why would I lie? I've told you the truth about the woman. I did not kill my…friends."

"Why should I believe you?"

"Why shouldn't you? I'm telling you the truth. Oh God, it's just occurred to me. If they're all dead, that means someone is out there still, they could be coming for me next. You can't let that happen. I don't want to die."

Katy hated this man. He was a snivelling wreck with no morals or remorse running through his veins. But, unfortunately, he had every right to receive protection from the murderer. However much that stuck in her craw. "Okay, I'll tell you what's going to happen. You're going to accompany us to the station where you're going to make a full confession to the murder of Sonia Crawford twenty-four years ago."

He sank into his chair and covered his head with his hands. "If that's what it takes to get you to protect me, then I'll do it."

"Do you need to collect anything or tell anyone you're coming with us?"

"I have no one. I live alone."

"Do you want to call your family solicitor or use the duty one at the station?"

"The duty one. Thank you. I'll just lock the back door."

"No, stay there where I can see you. DC Simpkins, will you do it, please?"

Charlie went through to the kitchen and nodded when she returned. "All done."

"Let's go then." Katy grabbed Pittman by the elbow and exited the house.

Charlie secured the front door behind them. Pittman was put in the back seat. Katy motioned for Patrick and Graham to go on ahead. Patrick gave her the thumbs-up and drew away slowly, waiting for Katy to get in the driver's seat and start up.

She followed Patrick back to the station but got cut off from him when the lights changed to red. "He'll wait up the road," she said to Charlie.

The car lunged forward. Katy hit her head on the steering wheel, and Charlie's forehead smashed into the dashboard.

"What the fuck is going on?" Pittman's panicked voice rifled around the inside of the car.

Dazed, Katy opened her car door and staggered out. A fist connected with her cheek, and she went down. The back door opened, and a screaming Pittman was yanked out of the car.

"He's mine. You're not taking him. I have plans for him."

Katy peered through the misty fog blurring her vision. "Who are you? No, you can't take him. He's our prisoner."

"He deserves to be punished for what he did."

"What did he do?" Katy tried to form her words into suitable sentences through the pain in her cheek. It was a struggle, but she just about managed it.

"Him and his mates, it was despicable the way he treated...week after week, year after year. No remorse whatsoever."

Katy peered up at the outline of the person, the sun blinding her, making it impossible to figure out who she was talking to. Car horns beeped as the lights changed colour.

Then the person ran, dragging the screaming Pittman with them back to their car.

"Charlie, are you all right?" Katy shouted.

"I think so."

"We have to help him."

"I know. I can't move, my head hurts so badly."

"Ring Patrick. Tell him what's going on. Call for help, Charlie." Katy struggled to get to her feet. It was imperative she didn't let this person get away. Her career would be on the line if she allowed that to happen. It gave her the impetus to get moving, to fight the fog of confusion surrounding her and go after the two of them.

The car pulled out from behind hers, and the driver put their foot down, heading straight towards her. Katy hit the ground and rolled out of the way. *Damn, they're getting away!*

A few hundred yards up the road, the sound of crunching metal and screeching tyres filled the air. Katy glanced up and was relieved to see Patrick and Graham tussling with the driver.

Charlie appeared before her. "Are you all right?"

Katy waved away her concern. "We have to find out who that person is, Charlie."

"The boys have the situation under control, and I've rung the station for backup. Let me help you up."

A couple of the drivers in nearby vehicles came to their assistance, better late than never, and helped them back to their car. Katy sat in the driver's seat for a second to catch her breath, but the pull to get involved proved too much. She staggered towards Patrick and Graham —she had to find out who this person was.

Patrick glanced up, his expression one of sheer horror and disbelief. "Tell her who you are," he ordered the mystery attacker.

"I'm the one he and his disgusting friends 'killed' all those years ago, except they didn't. I survived. I crawled out of the grave and survived." Tears ran down the woman's face. "I've come back to avenge my 'death' and what they put me through. No one can blame me for killing them. Ridding the world of such evil. I took pleasure in seeing their horrified expressions, thinking that a ghost had come back to finish them off."

Katy was rendered dumbstruck. Of all the conclusions they'd thought of, this wasn't one of them.

"Do your daughters know you're alive?"

"No. I've watched them both from afar for the last few months. I've been tempted a number of times to make myself known to them but was worried how they would take the news. I was determined to carry out my plan first and then I had every intention of revealing the truth to them."

"Why? After all these years, why start killing these men now?"

Her head dipped. "For years I've lived with amnesia. In one way, I wish I'd never recovered, and yet in another, I'm glad I did. Those men deserved to die. They should have been punished long ago. Why weren't they punished? Why did the truth never come out?"

"Because you're right, they were all cowards. Pittman admitted his life had been ruined by the events of that night..."

"Not enough for him to come forward to the police and reveal the truth, though."

"That's true. As much as I want to slap you on the back for what you've achieved this past week, I can't do it. These men shouldn't have died at your hands, they warranted being banged up for the rest of their lives. I'll ensure that happens to Pittman, you have my word on that."

"I did it for my girls. All of this was done so my girls no longer had to live in fear. I'm sure these men would have abused them the way they'd forced themselves upon me time and time again."

"You're wrong. The group split up after they thought they'd killed you, although both of your daughters have told me that their father abused them over the years."

"The bastard. That man was full of hatred for me. After the birth of Penny, my youngest, he turned on me, all because I'd neglected in my duties to reward him with a son. I told him we could try again, have another child, but he didn't want to take the risk of having yet another daughter. I tried to fend him off every night, took the beatings handed out to me, in the hope that he wouldn't take his anger out on the girls, and then he upped the ante, invited his friends to become involved in vile sex acts." A stream of tears fell, and her legs gave way beneath her.

Patrick broke her fall.

"All right, that's enough. Let's get her back to the station, boys. She can tell us the rest later," Katy muttered.

"What about you and Charlie, boss?" Patrick asked.

"Leave Pittman with us. Backup is on the way. We'll get my car recovered and hitch a ride with uniform. Treat her well, Patrick, she's been through hell."

He nodded and helped Sonia to her feet and into the back of the car.

EPILOGUE

The next few hours flew past in a torrent of emotions. Katy charged Amy and then set her free, promising to see her in court for her part in covering up the heinous crime all these years. Then Katy took the decision to call Nadia with a request for the young woman to join her at the station.

Nadia showed up, fearing the worst. "Please, I know you're going to arrest me, Inspector. How many times do I have to tell you? I had nothing to do with these murders. I'm mourning the loss of my father right now."

"I know that. Please, don't misconstrue why I've asked you to come here today. I want to reassure you that I now believe you weren't involved in the killing spree."

"That's brilliant. Does this mean you've caught the killer?"

Katy's throat suddenly clogged up. She swallowed, trying to shift the lump which had formed. "Yes. Oh God, I have some news for you and I'm not sure how you're going to react to it."

Nadia frowned and inclined her head. "What news?"

"Come with me." She led Nadia down the corridor to Interview Room Two and entered it. Sitting at the table were Charlie and Sonia. Sonia slowly turned to face her daughter.

Nadia shook her head and glanced at Katy. "I don't understand, who is she?"

Katy fought back the tears and whispered, "She's your mother, love."

Nadia's gaze swiftly shifted back to Sonia. "That's impossible... what kind of sick joke is this? My mother died that night...I saw what those men did to her..."

Sonia stood and held out her arms. "I'm sorry you had to witness that, my darling. It is me, I swear it is."

"But... but...they killed you?"

"They thought they had, they were idiots, they couldn't even do that properly."

"If what you're telling me is true, where have you been all these years?"

"Someone took me in, helped me to rediscover who I was. I had amnesia up until a few months ago. The psychiatrist told me that it was the mind's defence mechanism, to block out all the bad things pertaining to my previous life. I only ever had two good things happen, that was giving birth to you and Penny."

Nadia sobbed and ran into her mother's outstretched arms. After a few minutes, she stepped back and asked, "Does this mean you're going to be taken from us all over again?"

"I'm sorry, I suppose it does. I couldn't let them get away with it, love. The thought of those bastards subjecting other women to the demoralising acts they made me go through... I just couldn't let them get away with it."

"I understand, Mum."

Sonia smiled and touched her daughter's face. "I've missed hearing you say that word."

"I've thought of you non-stop over the years. I love you."

"Believe me, there's no greater love than a mother's love. How's your sister?"

Nadia gasped. "Oh God, she's going to be blown away by this news. I need to contact her."

"All in good time, sweetheart."

"Yes, all in good time. I'm sorry to have to break this reunion up, but we need to get on." Katy smiled apologetically at the two women clutching each other's hands.

"Just five more minutes," Nadia pleaded.

"DC Simpkins, we'll go grab a cup of coffee and leave these two ladies to get reacquainted for five minutes."

Sonia smiled at Katy. "Thank you."

Two female constables were stationed outside.

"I don't think they'll be any trouble, just keep an eye on them. We'll be back in ten minutes."

"Yes, ma'am," the blonde officer replied.

Walking upstairs to the incident room, Charlie asked, "Is that wise? Leaving them alone like that?"

"I think so. Sometimes you have to trust your gut on these things, Charlie."

"I suppose. God only knows how Penny is going to react to the news."

"After the initial shock, I'm sure she'll be thrilled to learn her mother is still alive."

"But she'll be banged up for the rest of her life…"

"True. They'll be able to visit her often, that's more than either of them could have wished for."

THE END

*W*ell that was another gripping investigation for Sara and her team to sink their teeth into. I hope you enjoyed it? If you did, then perhaps you'll consider leaving a review as they brighten an author's darkest days when imposter syndrome strikes.

. . .

Would you also consider reading another of my most popular series? Grab the first book in the Justice series, CRUEL JUSTICE

DI Sara Ramsey will return with a brand new case early in 2021.

KEEP IN TOUCH WITH THE AUTHOR

Newsletter
http://smarturl.it/8jtcvv

BookBub
www.bookbub.com/authors/m-a-comley

Blog
http://melcomley.blogspot.com

Join my special Facebook group to take part in monthly giveaways.

Readers' Group

Printed in Poland
by Amazon Fulfillment
Poland Sp. z o.o., Wrocław

62856286R00117